The Delaware Detectives:

# I Once
# Was Lost

Dana Rongione

# The Delaware Detectives:
# I Once Was Lost

*Book 4*
*The Delaware Detectives Mystery Series*

Published by
**A Word Fitly Spoken Press**

# Acknowledgements

This book would not have been possible without the help and support of the following people:

**The Lord, my Strength and Song** — Without Him, I can do nothing!

**My husband, Jason**

**My loyal and high-ranking patrons:**
> Lewis and Sharon White
> Patty Hicks
> Dawn Hodge
> Jo Anne Hall
> Peter Santaniello
> Lisa Gutschow
> Tara Looper
> And others who wish to remain anonymous. . .

**The Delaware Detectives Launch Team:**
> Nicole LaBrocca
> Aaron & Alaya Looper (real life brother and sister team who adore the *Delaware Detective Series*)
> Tamatha Redmond
> Kathleen Meacham

And last but not least, herbal tea.  Yes, I realize it isn't a person, but without it, I don't know if I would have made it through.   Praise the Lord for green tea, chamomile, ginger and peppermint!

# Table of Contents

# CHAPTER ONE

## Let the Games Begin

Jamie stood in the middle of our grandfather's backyard, dressed in what could only be described as a Halloween costume gone very wrong. An old football helmet concealed his mop of brown hair. His scrawny body looked to be three times its normal size thanks to the two bed pillows strapped to his stomach and back with duct tape. His arms and legs were wrapped in small blankets, again attached with duct tape. And on his hands, he wore oven mitts.

"What are you doing?" I asked my brother.

At the sound of my voice, the bundle of bed clothes jumped and turned in my direction. "Oh, Abby. You scared me. Don't sneak up on me like that. I am training Watson to be an attack dog."

My gaze shifted to the large dog lying on his back in the grass and wagging his tail as if to say, "Please rub my tummy."

"He doesn't look like much of an attack dog to me," I commented.

"Not yet," Jamie said, "but we've only started our training. Just wait and see. Before long, he'll be a ferocious[1] attack dog that any thief, drug dealer or smuggler would be terrified of."

Based on the description of bad guys that Jamie had given, it was safe to assume that he felt threatened as a part of the Delaware Detectives. True, we had taken on some cases that ended up being much more dangerous than we could have anticipated, but I had no idea that

Jamie had become afraid enough to feel the need to have an attack dog with us at all times. It would seem that there was more going on in my little brother's head than I knew about, and I wondered if we should leave the detective work to the professionals. After all, at only eight years old, it's only natural for Jamie to have a few fears.

"Abby, watch what Watson can do." Jamie held his right arm out in front of him and began to growl at the playful dog before him. "Attack!" Jamie screamed, all the while circling Watson who eyed him warily. "Attack! Attack!" At this final command, Watson rose and made a lunge toward Jamie, knocking him to the ground with his weight and strength. Standing beside my brother's fallen figure, Watson proceeded to lick him until my brother convulsed[2] in giggles and pushed the dog away. I could hardly contain my laughter, but I held myself together long enough to help Jamie up.

Once on his feet, Jamie dusted the grass from his ridiculous costume and shook his head at Watson who had resumed his belly-rub position on the grass. "I thought dogs were supposed to be smart, but I'm not so sure about this one."

Placing my hand on Jamie's padded shoulder, I replied, "Just give it time. Like you said, this was your first practice. I'm sure he'll get it. After all, you're a very good teacher."

Jamie smiled. "Thanks, Abby."

"Would you like to go to the library with me? Scott and Phyllis are coming too. We are going to do some more research on Nathanael Greene to see if we can figure out the combination to open the secret compartment in the desk."

Jamie's face brightened. "Count me in!"

I was impressed. This was the first time my brother had shown any interest in actually doing research at the library, which is not to say that he's not very good at it. Jamie is just the sort of person who would rather watch television or play video games than sit down and read a book.

"I think these codes and secret compartments are really cool," he confided. "In fact, I want to see if the library has some books on codes and ciphers and things like that. Do you think they will have that kind of thing?"

Shrugging my shoulders, I replied, "I really have no idea, but there's one way we can find out."

---

Before we go any further, I should probably fill you in on a couple of facts in case you haven't kept up with our adventures. My name is Abby Patterson. My brother, Jamie, and I are spending the summer in

Delaware with our grandfather, who we call Pop-Pop. Over the past couple of months, we have helped the police solve a couple of crimes, find a missing man, oh, and we discovered a hidden treasure. These adventures have earned us the name, *The Delaware Detectives*.

Along the way, we've met some new friends. Scott and Phyllis Hicks live down the street from Pop-Pop's enormous house. I guess you could say that we stumbled upon them during our first detective case while searching for a hidden fortune, but that's a story you'll have to read for yourself. Scott is—well—quite handsome with his swept-back blonde hair and deep green eyes. He also happens to be fourteen years old, just like me. Oddly enough, Phyllis is Jamie's age, though her lopsided auburn pigtails and small frame make her look younger.

It didn't take long for us to become fast friends, and we've worked together on two of the three cases we've solved while being here in Delaware. Jamie and I also adopted a stray dog, who we decided to call Watson (you know, like Sherlock Holmes' sidekick).

During our last case, I was fortunate enough to find an old campaign desk that once belonged to Nathanael Greene. In case you don't know who that is, Nathanael Greene was a Revolutionary war hero and good friends with George Washington. We discovered his campaign desk at an antique store, and with my parents permission, I bought it for myself. I absolutely love history!

As we were setting up the desk at Pop-Pop's house, Jamie discovered numbers on the bottoms of the drawers, which he believed to be some kind of combination to open a secret compartment within the desk. Based on the knowledge that Nathanael Greene was a known Freemason, and that the Freemasons of his time were very private and used many secret codes and ciphers, I believe Jamie may be right. Since the desk has four drawers, we assumed that the combination is likely a year, so it is my hope that we will find the information we need at the library.

If there's anything else you need to know, I'll try to fill you in along the way. For now, let's get into the story.

# CHAPTER TWO
## The Impossible Task

At the library, we divided into groups of two. Scott and I scanned the main section of the library, looking for books, articles and any other material we could dig up about Nathanael Greene. Jamie and Phyllis searched the Internet using the library's computers. The systems were old and quite slow, but they got the job done.

The library had many books about the Revolutionary War, but most of them didn't go into much detail about the particular soldiers and commanders that took part in the war. As for books specifically about Nathanael Greene, the selection was small, but we hoped it would be sufficient to meet our needs. Outside of those few books, the library didn't have any other sources of information about the famous Revolutionary War hero, not even in the reference section.

After finding all the books we could, Scott and I joined Jamie and Phyllis at the computers. Both of them were alternating between staring at the bright monitors and scribbling notes in the spiral notebooks I had insisted they bring.

"Did you guys find anything?" I whispered.

Jamie glanced at me over his shoulder. "Sure did. There's a lot of information online. In fact, there's too much for us to write down everything. What exactly are we looking for?"

"Well," Scott said, "from what Abby has told me, you expect the combination in the desk to be a year, right?"

"That would make the most sense," Jamie replied, "but we can't know for sure."

"Assuming it is a year," I interrupted, "it's most likely a year that was important to Greene, like maybe a birthday or anniversary."

"I found this list here," Phyllis spoke up, pointing to the screen in front of her. It's a long list of important dates in the life of Nathanael Greene. I'll go ask the librarian if she'll print it for us. There are a lot of dates there, and my hand is starting to cramp."

Phyllis pushed back her chair and stood, glancing once more at the computer screen. While she was speaking with the librarian, Jamie continued his online search while Scott and I stood behind him, peering over his shoulder. Within a few moments, Phyllis returned, printed pages in hand. Looking up at Scott, she said, "You'll need to pay the librarian. It cost fifty cents to print these out."

"Why don't you pay?" Scott asked.

Phyllis hung her head, her auburn pigtails stretching down past the tops of her shoulders. "Because I didn't bring any money with me."

"I'll take care of it," I said. "After all, you are both helping to solve a mystery about my desk. In fact, y'all deserve more of a reward than just that. How about we finish up here and then get some lunch, my treat?"

"Sounds good to me," Phyllis beamed. "Thanks, Abby."

"You don't have to do that, you know?" Scott remarked as he stared into my eyes.

"I know I don't have to, but I want to. Come on, it'll be fun!"

"Wait just a minute, guys!" Jamie yelled, then immediately lowered his voice when he noticed the librarian glaring at him. "I want to check and see if they have any books on codes and ciphers. Please, Abby. You said I could."

"Sure, Jamie. I'm sorry, I forgot. Do you want us to help you look?"

"That would be great," Jamie answered.

It didn't take us long to find the section that housed the books we were looking for, and Jamie was delighted to find that there were actually quite a number of books on secret codes. Picking out the ones that looked the most interesting to him, Jamie loaded up his arms with books of all sizes and headed happily toward the checkout counter. In fact, I can honestly say it was the happiest I had ever seen Jamie in regards to a book. Movies? Sure. Video games? Absolutely. But books? Not so much. Not Jamie anyway.

After paying the fee for the printed copies and checking out the books we had gathered, we strolled down to the Main Street Diner. It was still early enough in the day that the restaurant wasn't busy. Settling into one of the corner booths, we picked up our menus and scanned the lunch options. After a few moments, we each decided to order a burger, fries and a milkshake. For the next twenty minutes, the only sounds I heard were those of the traffic buzzing by on the busy street just outside the restaurant.  From the silence at our booth, I could only assume that my colleagues were either really hungry or deep in thought, as I was.

With our hunger satisfied and the bill paid, we made our way back to Pop-Pop's house and hurried to my upstairs bedroom where we could begin trying out different date combinations. It seemed a bit silly. After all, we had no idea if there was a secret compartment in the desk. We could be jumping to conclusions and getting worked up about something that wasn't even real. Still, we didn't have anything better to do, so where was the harm?

For the next few hours, we tried every year we could come up with. We experimented with the year of Greene's birth, his marriage, and even his children's births. We tested various dates that pertained to the war, like the year it began, the year it ended and even the year he was made quartermaster. But nothing happened. No secret drawer popped out. Indeed, it was truly beginning to feel like a waste of time.

"How do we know we've got the drawers in the right order?" Scott asked from his reclined position on the floor.

I shifted on the bed and set aside the book that had been lying in my lap. "What do you mean?"

"Well, we've been assuming that the first number is the top drawer, the second one is the left drawer, the third one is the small middle drawer, and the last number is the drawer on the right. In other words, we've been thinking from left to right. But what if the numbers were top to bottom? Then, the two middle drawers would come first, then the two bottom drawers. You see what I mean?"

I studied the desk. It was possible that Scott was on to something though it didn't seem very likely. Looking at the desk, it seemed to me that our initial order was the most probable one, but since we weren't making any progress, I figured it wouldn't hurt to try.

We spent another hour or so going through the various dates again, but this time in the order that Scott had suggested. Nothing! No secret compartment. No hidden drawer. Absolutely nothing!

"Oh man! We've got to go," Phyllis groaned, looking toward the oval clock on the wall. "Our mom will kill us if we're late for dinner."

# CHAPTER THREE

## A Stroll Through History

The next morning, I dressed and shuffled downstairs to fix breakfast. I was startled to find my grandfather sitting at the table in the large dining room just off the kitchen. After glancing at the clock, I asked, "Pop-Pop, what are you doing here? I thought you would be at work by now."

Pop-Pop peeked over the top edge of the newspaper he was reading and smiled. "Well, I thought that since you kids were going home in another week or so that it would be nice to spend a little more time with you. The summer has gone by too fast. I decided to take the day off work so we could all do something together."

"Really?" I exclaimed. For the past few weeks, Pop-Pop had been filling in for an employee who had been injured on the job, and during that time, we had hardly seen him except for in the evenings and on Sundays when we all went to church together. While I certainly understood his need to work, Jamie and I had missed the time with him.

Pop-Pop folded his newspaper and laid it to the side. "What would you kids like to do?"

I ran through a list of ideas in my head, but one stood out above the rest. "Well, Jamie and I have been trying to figure out if there's a secret compartment in my new desk. So far, we haven't had any luck, but we were thinking that we might be able to find some clues at another antique store. The desk came from Mr. Reed's antique shop, and he told me that the desk was actually part of a set. There's also a bookcase that goes with it, but Mr. Reed hasn't been able to locate it. If we could find the bookcase, maybe we could figure out the combination to the desk."

Pop-Pop nodded, looking deep in thought. Making his way to the kitchen, he began pulling various dishes from the cabinets. As he grabbed the bacon and eggs from the refrigerator, he turned back to face me. "I'd be happy to take you around to some antique stores, but I hope you realize that the chances of actually finding that bookcase are slim. I mean, it could have already been sold or sent to another part of the country. I just don't want you to get your hopes up."

After pouring myself a glass of orange juice, I sat down at the table. "I won't, Pop-Pop. I know it's a long shot, but the way I see it, visiting the antique stores will be fun either way. You know how much I love old stuff."

"What about your brother?"

True, Jamie was typically as excited about history as he was about reading, but something had come over him during the past couple of weeks. Between the stuff we learned about the Lenape Indians and the information we'd gathered about the Revolutionary War, he seemed to be taking more of an interest in the past. He was especially fascinated with the Freemasons and their use of codes and secret messages.

"I think he'll enjoy it too, but we can ask him when he gets up."

Sure enough, Jamie was all for it, so after breakfast, we piled into Pop-Pop's old truck and headed toward the city. As I was getting ready, I thought about asking Pop-Pop if we could invite Scott and Phyllis, but I quickly abandoned[3] the idea. If Pop-Pop wanted to spend time with us, it wouldn't really be fair to invite others to come along. As much as I enjoyed Scott and Phyllis's company, I was looking forward to a day spent with just the three of us. Watson, of course, had to stay home, but he had grown content with his many new toys and chew treats.

The drive into the city only took about fifteen minutes. According to Pop-Pop, the cities of Wilmsboro and Dunn were home to several antique shops which prided themselves in unique historical goods. The first store we stopped at was called *Seasoned Stuff.* It was a gray block building in the shape of a triangle. One of the points of the triangle was the entrance, at which stood a huge wooden door that reminded me of something out of medieval times. It was huge and ornate, making me feel small and plain as I stood before it.

As soon as we stepped through the door, we encountered what appeared to be an obstacle course. Furniture of all shapes and sizes was stacked and crammed into nearly every available space. I immediately felt claustrophobic and inched forward through the narrow space between the piles of stuff.

"Oh my," was all that Pop-Pop could say.

Jamie, however, was not at a loss for words. "This place is a mess!"

As I rounded the first corner of antiques, I spied a plump, middle-aged woman with short blonde hair and wire-rimmed glasses. She was sitting at a huge desk that occupied much of the right-hand side of the store. She looked up, smiled and said, "Good morning." Then she went back to studying the papers in front of her.

We continued to wind our way through the maze of vintage dressers, large mirrors, coffee tables, gaudy[4] lamps and much more. With each step, it seemed less likely that we would find what we were looking for. For the most part, the items were old but not two hundred or more years old. As I tilted my head back to admire a grandfather clock, I noticed the ceiling, which was made of hundreds of silver beaded tiles that reflected the light around the room. Unfortunately, other than an interesting coffee table that contained a uniquely-colored map of the world, the shiny ceiling was the most interesting part of the store.

The second antique store was about the same size as the first but was much more of a traditionally square-shaped building. It's gray brick with black trim gave it a gloomy and run-down feel, especially since there was some sort of green plant growing up the side of the building. Bright red letters floated above the double doorway.

"Checkered Past," Jamie read aloud, then giggled. "That's a funny name for a store."

I had to agree, but once we entered the shop, it all made sense. Black-and-white tiles covered the floors in a checkered pattern, reminding me of a gigantic chess board. A quick scan around the room brought to mind pictures and television shows I've seen of 50s diners. The walls were covered with old movie posters, license plates and funny quotes. A juke box sat in one corner, an old gasoline pump in another. Without a doubt, I knew we were in for an eclectic[5] assortment of old goods. Fortunately, unlike the previous antique shop, this one seemed to be neat and orderly.

Turning to our left, we began making our way up and down the aisles. The shop seemed to have a little bit of everything. There were dishes, pocket knives, vintage clothing, army gear and just about every collectible you could think of from vinyl records to thimbles. Once again, however, none of the pieces seemed to date back to the 18th century. I stopped to admire an ornate dresser with a large mirror attached. Staring at my reflection, I noticed that the mirror had some sort of film or covering on it that made my dull brown eyes and matching hair appear somewhat orange. I couldn't help but laugh at the sight. I'd never thought of myself as a clown, but maybe I could pull it off.

"Look at these!" Jamie called out from the opposite side of the shop.

Pop-Pop was busy talking with the storeowners – a husband and wife team if I had to guess – so I strode over to see what Jamie had found. He was standing in front of a tall glass case that displayed a variety of coins. At first, I couldn't figure out why Jamie would be so excited about coins. After all, he'd never been interested in them before. But after glancing at the coins again, two of them caught my attention.

"They're Mason coins," Jamie declared. "Look, see the symbols there? I recognize them from the books I've been reading. Those are definitely some of the symbols from the Freemasons."

"Yep, that's pretty cool."

"I'm going to buy them," Jamie said excitedly.

I looked at the case again and noticed that each of the coins had been marked down from nine dollars to six dollars. Not a bad price for a little piece of history. About that time, Pop-Pop came over to see what we were looking at. After Jamie explained to him the significance of the coins, he asked the owner to open the case so that Jamie could take a better look. Once they were in his hands, my brother studied the coins, flipping them over and turning them side to side to read the inscriptions.

"Yep, I definitely want them!" Jamie shouted, bouncing up and down the way he did when he was excited.

After paying, we left the store and visited a couple of other shops. They were both very fancy and featured items like glass chandeliers and oil paintings. In a way, they reminded me more of museums than antique stores. After not finding anything of interest in either of those shops, we stopped for lunch and then decided to try one more place that the waitress told us about. It was a huge antique mall called *Oldie's Antiques*.

# CHAPTER FOUR

## The Mystery Within a Mystery

The sprawling white building reminded me of an airplane hangar because of its size and design. Red letters spelled out the name Oldie's Antiques. (What was it about antique shops and red letters?) A double glass door was the only opening into the store. There were no windows or other doors that I could see, though I assumed there was at least a back door of some sort.

As soon as we walked through the door, we came to a sign that read, "For your protection and ours, please place all purses, backpacks and other bags in the lockers to your left." I turned and noticed the row of lockers much like those we had in school, only smaller. Several of the doors were closed, indicating that they were in use. The other doors stood open, their keys in place in the locks. As I pulled my emergency bag over my shoulder, I noticed another sign over the lockers which read, "Please leave your bags here. Once your items are secured in the locker, lock the door and take the key with you. Be sure not to lose it if you want to reclaim your items."

"I'm not sure how good I feel about leaving my bag up here," I said, "but I guess if everything is locked up and I have the key, it should be safe enough."

I chose one of the bottom lockers and shoved my bag inside.

"Wait a second, Abby," Jamie called. He was digging in his pants pocket for something, no doubt the two Mason coins he had bought earlier. "Will you put these in your bag too? I don't want to lose them, and I certainly don't want anyone to think that I stole them."

I took the coins from him (and let me tell you, they were a lot heavier than I expected) and placed them in the small inside pocket of my bag. After returning the bag to the locker, I closed the door and grabbed the key which had a small chain on it. I quickly discovered that the chain slipped easily over my wrist, allowing me to wear the key as a bracelet. We had only taken a couple of steps when a tall, broad-shouldered man came forward to greet us. Casually dressed in jeans and a nice button up shirt, he reminded me a lot of my uncle, though definitely a bit older judging by his gray-streaked hair and bifocals.

"Good afternoon," he said in a pleasant voice as he shook Pop-Pop's hand. "How can I help you folks today?"

Pop-Pop returned the smile. "We'd just like to look around for a bit if that's okay."

"Absolutely," the man replied. "Let me tell you a bit about the store. My name is Mr. Oldie. I am the owner of this establishment."

Jamie snickered and leaned over to whisper in my ear. "Mr. Oldie owns an antique store. That's like a preacher being named Mr. Lord!" I couldn't help but join in with Jamie's giggles. After all, he did have a good point.

Ignoring our behavior, Mr. Oldie continued. "This antique mall is unlike any other in the area. We have exhibits and collections from several different vendors. You'll see their identification numbers on the walls and shelves above their displays. We have the widest assortment of antiques for miles around and even have items dating back as far as the 1700s."

Now he had my attention!

"All of the items within the store are priced. If you have any questions, please feel free to ask."

At that moment, Mr. Oldie turned to look at Jamie and me. His nose turned up as if he smelled something rotten. Focusing his attention on Pop-Pop once again, he continued, "We do ask that you do not allow the children to play with any of the items in the store. In fact, it would be best if they didn't touch anything at all."

Pop-Pop frowned slightly but spoke in a polite manner. "I'm sure we won't have any problems."

The store was so large, we didn't know where to begin, so we strolled past the lockers and started walking the many aisles. Mr. Oldie had not exaggerated. His shop had a little bit of everything. It took us nearly two hours to walk the aisles on the left side of the store, so we quickened our pace a bit as we hit the center section, stopping occasionally to take a closer look at something that caught our attention.

"Abby, you've got to see this!" Jamie shouted from one aisle over. Noticing nothing else of interest in the current aisle, I hurried over to my brother. When I found him, my mouth dropped open. He was standing next to Nathanael Greene's campaign desk – my desk!

"What in the world?" I muttered.

The desk was identical to mine in every respect except that it didn't look quite as beat up. Tilting my head from side to side, I tried to understand how my desk could have a twin.

At that moment, Pop-Pop shuffled over. "What did you kids find?" Before we could answer, he spotted the desk and said, "Well, I'll be."

"How can it be the same desk?" Jamie asked.

Pop-Pop stroked his chin. "Well, didn't you kids say that Greene took part in the war from the beginning to the end?"

Jamie and I nodded.

"That was a long time. It's possible he had more than one campaign desk during that time. Don't you think?"

"I guess so," I said, "but don't you think it's strange that it looks exactly the same? Besides, Mr. Reed said that this desk and a matching bookcase were made specifically for General Greene. He never said anything about a second desk. Something seems off here."

Jamie snapped his fingers, startling me. "I know. I bet it's like the twin Resolute desks."

"The what?" Pop-Pop and I asked together.

"A long time ago, an important ship named the *Resolute* got stuck in a bunch of ice, and the crew had to abandon the ship. Years later, the ship was found, and some craftsmen used the wood to make two identical desks. One of them is in Buckingham Palace, and the other one is in the Oval Office of the White House. Maybe your desk has a twin too."

I stared in amazement. How was it possible that my brother knew this vital piece of history when this was the first I'd heard of it? Unable to contain my curiosity, I had to ask, "How in the world do you know about the twin Resolute desks?"

Jamie smiled, obviously pleased with his knowledge. "I saw it on a movie once."

Pop-Pop sighed. "Oh, Jamie. How many times must I tell you that you can't always believe everything you see on television? The writers of the movie could have made all of that up. You might want to check your facts before you claim them as truth."

"I know, Pop-Pop. I don't know if it's true or not, but it is possible, right?" Squatting down on the floor, Jamie leaned under the desk.

"What are you doing?" I whispered, looking around to make sure nobody was watching us.

"I want to see if this one has numbers on the bottom of the drawers like yours does."

"Well, hurry up and be careful."

Jamie slid open each drawer, shaking his head repeatedly. After closing the final drawer, he stood up, dusting off his clothes. "Nope. No numbers."

At that moment, Mr. Oldie appeared out of nowhere. "Ah, I see you've discovered one of our treasures. You know, that desk belonged to General Nathanael Greene who fought in the Revolutionary War."

Pop-Pop threw a look at both of us – a look that clearly said, "Keep quiet."

"Is that so?" Pop-Pop said. "I don't suppose you have the matching bookcase, do you? As I understand, it was a set."

Mr. Oldie paled and stammered for a moment. "The bookcase? Um, no, I'm afraid we don't have that piece. We were fortunate to find the desk. After all, you can't really find pieces like this anymore."

Jamie and I exchanged glances. Something was definitely not right with this place or Mr. Oldie, for that matter.

As the owner hurried off to help another customer, Pop-Pop turned to us, his eyebrows raised. "Suspicious fellow, isn't he? Perhaps we'd better go on home."

"Please, can we finish looking?" I pleaded. As much as Mr. Oldie gave me the creeps and the desk made me confused, I didn't want to miss out on the opportunity to see more history. I may not trust the owner, but he did have a fascinating collection."

Pop-Pop looked at his watch. "Another hour, no more, so you'd better look quickly."

---

After leaving *Oldie's Antiques*, we stopped by a pizza place and picked up a couple of pizzas for our dinner. As we drove, the smell of bacon and pepperoni tickled my nose and caused my stomach to cry out with embarrassing noises. How had I not realized that I was so hungry?

Once in the house, Pop-Pop sent us upstairs to wash up for dinner. Dropping my emergency bag on the bed, I flopped down and removed my worn tennis shoes. Just as I was about to make my way to the bathroom, Jamie entered my room through the doorway that connected the two upstairs bedrooms.

"May I have my coins back? I want to take a look at them."

I gestured to my bag as I headed out the door. "They're in the small inside pocket. Just don't touch anything else."

Jamie grabbed the bag and tore into it like a starving man tearing into a picnic lunch. "I don't see them," he cried.

With the aroma of pizza climbing the stairs and calling for my attention, I was tempted to ignore my brother's whines, but I knew that was rude. Besides, I didn't want him to rip my bag apart looking for his crazy coins. Returning to the bedside, I snatched the bag from him and searched the inside pocket. The coins weren't there.

"Maybe they fell out somehow," I mumbled as I turned the bag upside down, emptying its contents onto the bed. After searching through my wild assortment of pens, bottled water, notepads, tissues and more, one thing became very clear: Jamie's coins had vanished!

# CHAPTER FIVE

## Retracing Our Steps

The next morning, we called Scott and Phyllis over to tell them about our adventures with Pop-Pop the day before and the duplicate desk we had found. We also filled them in on the disappearance of Jamie's new coins.

"Would it be okay if we borrowed your bikes again today?" I asked Scott. "Pop-Pop said we could go back to the city to retrace our steps from yesterday and see if we can find Jamie's coins, but he has to work until late this afternoon. He told us it would be okay if we went on our own as long as we had some transportation. He's not comfortable with us walking that far."

"Sure," Scott answered. "We could all go together if you don't mind the company."

*I never mind your company*, I thought, then blushed. "Um, yes, of course."

"Can Watson come too?" Jamie pleaded. "He'd love to get outside for a while."

I eyed the dog who was stretched out on the braided rug in the middle of my bedroom floor. As Jamie stroked his head, Watson's eyes closed in contentment. It amazed me how that same dog had been tearing through the house only moments before, and now he was nearly asleep. That's a dog's life, I guess.

"I'd love to, Jamie, but I don't think it would be a good idea. He won't be allowed in any of the shops, which means someone will have to stay outside with him at every stop. Do you want to do that?"

Jamie continued to stroke the now-snoring dog. "No, I guess not."

"How about we take him to the park when we're done, okay?"

Jamie nodded in agreement.

After collecting the bikes from Scott and Phyllis's house, we headed out. Fortunately, the towns were very easy to navigate, so we didn't need to ask for directions. Besides, I have a pretty good memory when it comes to things like directions and maps.

As planned, our first stop was *Oldie's Antiques*. It seemed likely that Jamie's coins fell out of my bag when I had stored it in the lockers. It shouldn't take long to figure out whether or not that was the case.

The shop didn't have a parking area for bicycles, so we hid them behind a row of hedges off to the side of the building and prayed they would still be there when we got back.

As soon as we entered the store, Mr. Oldie approached. "What do you kids want?"

Scott and Phyllis stepped back, leaving Jamie and me to face the grouchy storeowner.

"We were here yesterday," I began, "and my brother lost something. We think they may have fallen out of my bag when I stored it in the lockers."

Mr. Oldie turned his attention to Jamie. "What did you lose, boy?"

Jamie gulped. "Uh, two Mason coins, sir. They were still in the package. I hadn't even had a chance to open them yet."

"Nope, no coins here. We check the lockers every night before closing to make sure no one has left anything. We didn't find any coins."

"Would it be okay if we took a look anyway?" I asked hesitantly.

The store owner harumphed. "There's no need, girly. I told you, we checked the lockers last night, and there were no coins." With his arms open wide, he began gently pushing us toward the door. "Now, if you'll excuse me, I'm a very busy man."

I saw the tears pooling in Jamie's eyes but decided not to mention them so I didn't embarrass him. I was tempted to give Mr. Oldie a piece of my mind, but fortunately, I remembered what the Bible teaches about respecting our elders. Still, it was hard to keep my thoughts to myself as we left the store.

"Now what?" Jamie squeaked.

"Now we follow our path from yesterday," I said.

And that's exactly what we did. We went back to every place we had been the day before: the antique stores, the deli where we had eaten lunch and even the pizza place. We looked around and spoke to the employees, but in the end, we still couldn't find Jamie's coins. It was like they truly had vanished.

"I knew it," Jamie sighed as we exited the library. "As soon as I get excited about anything, something bad happens. It's just not fair, Abby."

I felt so badly for my poor brother. I don't think I had ever seen him so discouraged. I knew he was excited about the coins, but I had no idea they meant so much to him. I wished, with all my heart, that there was something I could do for him. Then suddenly, I had a great idea.

"Let's go see Mr. Reed. He may have some Mason coins or, at the very least, may know where we can find some."

Jamie's face brightened. "Abby, you're the best sister ever!"

# CHAPTER SIX
## An Old Friend

The ride to *Reed's Antiques* was fairly long, and I prayed the entire way that this wouldn't be another dead end. The little bell over the door tinkled as the four of us entered the shop. The owner—wearing a long-sleeved, plaid shirt and sweater vest despite the heat of the day—stood behind the counter, studying some treasure with the aid of a magnifying glass. The glaring overhead lights cast shadows across his face but didn't do much to hide the wrinkles of his aged skin. At the sound of the bell, he looked up.

"Why, if it isn't my favorite group of detectives!" His smile was warm and friendly, a stark contrast[6] to the angry frown of Mr. Oldie.

We first met Mr. Reed a few weeks ago at a meeting to preserve a piece of land that used to belong to the Lenape Indians.   Mr. Reed, a descendent of the Lenapes, has been heavily involved in the effort to keep the land from being sold and turned into a shopping plaza. Unfortunately, the county hasn't made a decision yet about what will happen to the property.

At first, I didn't trust Mr. Reed. Though he looked kindly enough, there was something suspicious about him, like he had many secrets to hide. But once we got to know the elderly man, we found him to be one of the nicest men in the world. He's like one of those people you feel like you've known forever even though you've only just met. A true friend through and through.

As we strode to the glass counter in the front corner of the old antique store, we explained to the shop owner about Jamie's missing coins and the reason for our visit. "So, we were wondering if you had any Mason coins."

Mr. Reed looked at Jamie sadly. "No, I'm afraid I don't have any here in the shop, but I could make some calls. I have connections with a lot of other dealers, I think there's a good chance I could track down some coins for you."

"Really?" Jamie shouted.

"Yes, really, but I'll need a few days to make all the calls. Can you come back at the end of the week?"

"Absolutely," Jamie replied.

Mr. Reed smiled again. "Good. Now, is there anything else I can help you kids with?"

I spoke up. "Actually, I was hoping I could ask you a question about the campaign desk."

"Ah, yes," Mr. Reed said, leaning on the counter and propping his head up with his hands. "What about it?"

"Do you have any idea how many desks Nathanael Greene actually had? I mean, he probably had several of them throughout the course of the war, right?"

"Strangely not," the storekeeper replied. "Through my research, I've discovered that Greene was the only general to use the same campaign desk throughout his entire enlistment. That's why he had it specifically commissioned, so that it could withstand the hardships of war. That's also why the desk is worth so much. It truly is one-of-a-kind."

Jamie and I exchanged glances with each other and then with Scott and Phyllis.

"Could it be like the Resolute desks?" Jamie blurted. "Could there be a twin to Greene's desk?"

Mr. Reed chuckled. "Ah, the Resolute desks. Now, that is a tale, but I'm afraid it's probably not the one you've heard. The fact is that there are no twin desks though that's not to say that part of the story isn't true. There was a ship called the *HMS Resolute*, and it did become ice-locked in a sea of glaciers. After it was recovered, the ship was dismantled and the wood used to make various artifacts under the order of Queen

Victoria. Among those artifacts were at least three different desks. Queen Victoria gifted the first one, which was a large, robust desk, to Rutherford B. Hayes. That is the desk that now resides in the Oval Office. The second desk was a much smaller, more feminine desk which looked nothing like the first. It is now housed in the Royal Naval Museum in England. The third desk was another small desk commissioned[7] as a gift for the widow of Henry Grinnell, the man who had funded the expeditions to find the *Resolute*. It now resides in the Whaling Museum. So, you see, the story of the twin Resolute desks is part fact and part fiction. Other than a lot of replicas that can be found in museums all over the world, there are no identical twin desks that came from the *Resolute*."

Poor Jamie looked heartbroken, and I couldn't blame him. It's discouraging to believe you know the truth about something only to find out that part of the story is not the truth at all. I would have dwelled on it more, but the question burning in my mind wasn't about the Resolute desks but rather Greene's campaign desk.

I cleared my throat. "So what would you say if I told you that we saw a desk identical to Greene's campaign desk at another antique store?"

Mr. Reed straightened. "I'd have to say that one of them is a fake."

"So, Mr. Oldie is selling fake antiques," Jamie mused.

At the mention of the name, the shop owner's eyes grew wide. "Oldie?" Mr. Reed questioned. "I wouldn't be surprised. I always thought there was something odd about him, but we mustn't jump to conclusions. Remember the trouble you got yourselves into the last time you made assumptions before you had all the facts?"

I knew he was referring to the time I accused him of trying to scare people away from Beaver Valley, the piece of land that once belonged to his ancestors, the ancient Lenape Indians. My face flushed at the memory.

"You're right," Scott said. "We need some proof."

Mr. Reed focused his eyes on each of us in turn. "Well, it's about time for my lunch break. How about I close the store, and I'll take a trip down to *Oldie's Antiques*? I should be able to tell if the items he's selling are true antiques or copies. You kids are welcome to join me, but you'll need to keep your suspicions in check. We don't want anyone to know we're there spying."

Not wanting to leave our bikes behind, the four of us decided to ride to *Oldie's Antiques* while Mr. Reed drove his car. Because of the various shortcuts we knew and our ability to avoid intersections and stoplights, we arrived at the store before he did. Stashing our bicycles once again in the bushes beside the building, we made our way to the front door where we waited for Mr. Reed. As we spotted his car turning into the parking lot, we entered the store.

Before the door had even closed behind us, we were met by Mr. Oldie. "What are you kids doing here again? I told you this morning that I couldn't help you."

At that moment, Mr. Reed came in behind us and cleared his throat. "These children are with me. I trust that's not a problem."

Mr. Oldie lowered his head slightly. "No, sir, of course not. I apologize if I came across rather rough. You can never be too careful with young people these days. Seems that most of them are nothing but a bunch of thieves."

Mr. Reed raised an eyebrow. "Is that so?"

A red flush began to rise from under Mr. Oldie's collar and crept up his face. "Not that I'm saying these young people are thieves. Please don't misunderstand me." The owner eyed me suspiciously, his glare sending chills up and down my spine. "That being said, girly, I will remind you that you'll need to place your bag in the lockers."

I clutched my emergency bag to my side, feeling uneasy about leaving it in the lockers as I had before. What if they had extra keys and could open up the locker when I wasn't looking? What if they went through my things? I looked to Mr. Reed who nodded slightly as if to say, "It will be fine. Just go along with it." Not wanting to cause a scene or to hinder[8] our investigation, I slipped my bag off my shoulder and placed it in one of the bottom lockers, removing the key from the lock and placing it on my wrist as I had done before.

"Is there anything in particular I can help you with today?" Mr. Oldie asked.

Mr. Reed stared from left to right, studying his surroundings. "If it's all right, we'd just like to look around for a bit. We'll let you know if we need anything."

The owner bowed slightly, "Very good, sir." And with that, he was off to parts unknown within the gigantic store.

"This place is huge," Mr. Reed said, still scanning the room and the variety of objects it contained. "It would probably be best if we split up. Jamie and Phyllis, why don't you two come with me? Scott and Abby, you two can check out the other side of the store."

Scott narrowed his eyes. "What exactly is it that we're looking for?"

"I'm not sure," said Mr. Reed, "but take note of anything that seems suspicious or off in any way."

Scott and I made our way toward the right hand side of the store where we walked the aisles, studying each and every item for anything that seemed irregular. Without really knowing what we were looking for and not understanding how to spot counterfeit antiques, it felt a bit like searching for a needle in a haystack, and I wasn't really sure if we were accomplishing what we had set out to do. Still, we did our best and tried to keep track of anything that looked odd, which would have been a lot easier if I could have used the notepad in my emergency bag that I had left in the lockers up front.

After about an hour or so, we met up with Jamie and Phyllis who had moved to the center section of the antique mall. "What are you guys doing here? I thought you were with Mr. Reed on the other side of the store."

"We were," Jamie said, "but Mr. Reed said that this place was so big that it would be better if we split up again, so he sent Phyllis and me to the center section of the store. But we found something we wanted to show you. Come with us."

Jamie and Phyllis turned and walked toward the back of the store where large glass display cases held a variety of items—everything from handguns to miniature teacups. The two stopped in front of one of the smaller cases, and I immediately recognized the contents. Without warning, frustration overwhelmed me. "Jamie, we're not here shopping for coins. We have a job to do, or have you forgotten?" I knew my words had come across harshly, but I was ashamed that Jamie could be so selfish to think about his stupid coins when it was very possible that Mr. Oldie was robbing people.

Either unaware or unmoved by my feelings, Jamie shook his head. "I'm not shopping for coins, but I admit I did stop to look. But that's when I noticed these." He pointed to two coins that sat on the bottom row of the glass enclosure.

Taking a step forward and squatting down to that level, I peered into the case and stared at the two Mason coins before me. I hadn't taken a good look at the coins that Jamie had bought the day before, so I couldn't say for sure, but to me, they looked like the same coins. Both were brown and only slightly shiny. The first one had the image of an open book in the center with a big eye above it and clasped hands underneath. The second bore the picture of a palm tree in the center along with the words *South Carolina* and several dates around the edge. Glancing up at Jamie, I noticed the confusion on his face. "Were these coins here yesterday?"

Jamie shook his head. "No, I'm positive they weren't. I checked all of these cases, and there weren't any Mason coins among them. I'm sure of it, Abby."

"Are you saying these are your coins?" Scott asked.

Jamie shrugged. "I can't be sure. After all, I didn't really get a chance to look at the coins very well yesterday before I lost them, but they do look familiar."

"Is there any way to find out if they are the same coins?" Phyllis asked, joining me in a crouched position on the floor.

"I'm not sure," I said, "but maybe they have some kind of an identification number or serial number or something that can be traced. Perhaps the store where Jamie bought them would have some information on them." Rising to my feet and steadying myself, I looked at Jamie. "If nothing else, if you go ahead and buy them, you'll have some Mason coins again."

With a decision made, Jamie and Phyllis went off in search of Mr. Reed, while Scott and I sought out Mr. Oldie to ask the owner to open the case containing the coins. As we walked toward the back corner of the store, we noticed a large black door bearing a sign that read "No Entry." Assuming the door led to some back office or possibly a stock room, I intended to walk right past it, but as we neared it, I noticed the door was ajar, and voices drifted out through the narrow opening. Scott and I paused, looking around to make sure no one was watching us.

"The delivery has to be tonight," said a rough voice. "The owners are eager to get rid of it, for obvious reasons."

"What if someone sees us? Won't people think it's odd that we're taking deliveries in the middle of the night?"

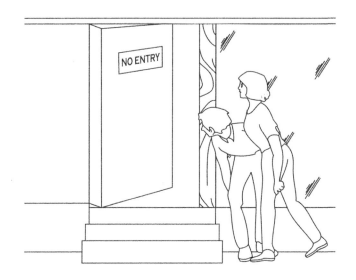

I couldn't be sure, but I was almost positive that the second voice belonged to Mr. Oldie.

"It's the only way," said the other voice. "It's too risky during the day. Besides, who's going to be around in the middle the night to see it anyway?"

The sound of chair legs screeching across the floor blended with foot steps that shuffled in our direction. Scott and I turned and hurriedly made our way out of sight. Peeking around a tall wooden dresser, I watched as Mr. Oldie exited the room, followed by a short, wiry man with greasy black hair and a thin mustache that reminded me of a skinny caterpillar. The two men made their way toward the front of the store, and I immediately let out the breath I didn't realize I had been holding.

"What was that all about?" Scott asked.

"I'm not sure, but I think we need to be at that meeting tonight."

# CHAPTER SEVEN
## Let's Talk Coins

After paying for Jamie's coins and collecting my bag from the lockers, we all met up around Mr. Reed's car to discuss our findings.

"I can't believe these cost twenty dollars a piece," Jamie complained as he studied the coins in his hands. "They were only six dollars at the other place."

Mr. Reed folded his arms over his chest and leaned back against his brown station wagon, eyeing the white building we had just exited. "There are definitely some odd things going on in there. Some of the stuff seems original, but I'm pretty sure I spotted some counterfeit items. Still, I would hate to accuse someone of a crime without having proof. I need to go back to my shop and do some research. Only then will I be able to confirm my suspicions, but if I'm right, Mr. Oldie is definitely a crook."

I followed Mr. Reed's gaze and then stared at Jamie's new coins. "Mr. Reed, do you know if there's a way to find out whether or not these are the same coins that Jamie bought yesterday?"

"They don't have any kind of number on them other than a few dates," Jamie said, turning the coins this way and that.

Mr. Reed held out his hand and took one of the coins from Jamie. Holding it close to his face and turning it into the sunlight, he studied both sides carefully. "You're right, Jamie, these don't seem to have a serial number, but that's not unusual for certain coins. Anytime I have an item in the store that doesn't have any kind of identifying mark, I always take a picture of it for inventory purposes. It's likely that the store you got them from does the same."

"Well, I guess I know where we're going next," Phyllis giggled.

"Yep," I nodded. "It's time to revisit *Checkered Past.*"

As we entered the gray building with black trim, I could see by their expressions that Scott and Phyllis were shocked by the inside of the building.

"This place is awesome," Scott said.

"Can we look around?" Phyllis asked, already making her way toward the costumes in the front corner.

"Y'all go ahead," I said. "Jamie and I will talk to the owners, and we'll meet up with you in a minute."

As the siblings wandered off, Jamie and I made our way to the counter, recognizing the man and woman whom we had met the day before. They smiled as the man rose from his seat and stepped up to greet us. "What can I do for you today?"

Jamie pulled the two coins from his pocket and set them on the counter. Immediately, I realized that we had failed to discuss how much information we should give this couple regarding *Oldie's Antiques*. After all, as Mr. Reed had stated, we didn't know for sure that he was doing anything wrong. Frantically searching my brain for a way to ask the question that we needed answered without casting blame on Mr. Oldie or sounding suspicious myself, I decided to go with the "less is more" option.

"We were just wondering if you had any way to track coins that you've sold… you know, for inventory purposes and stuff," I blurted.

The man twisted his mouth to one side and tilted his head to the opposite side. "Well, I must say, that's a very grown-up question. To answer it, yes, we often track coins by their serial numbers. We list each of the numbers in a ledger, along with where we got the coin, when we got it, when it sold and how much it sold for. Does that answer your question?"

"What if they don't have serial numbers?" Jamie asked. "Like these." He pushed the coins forward, and the owner picked them up one at a time, studying them carefully.

Nodding, he placed the coins back in Jamie's palm and spoke. "In that case, we take a picture of the item and place it in the ledger, along with all the other information."

Jamie and I exchanged glances, uncertain how to continue. The ticking of the second hand on the clock just above the counter indicated the passing of time as I wondered what to say next. Before I could think of anything, Jamie spoke. "Could you look at your ledger and see if these are the two coins that I bought from you yesterday?"

The man looked puzzled, and I was certain he was going to ask for more information or to question why we wanted to know, but instead, he shrugged and turned away, shuffling over to a small desk in the corner. Pulling a thick leather book from a narrow shelf, he sat down in the chair and began thumbing through the pages. His finger traced a line down each page until it reached a place where it stopped, and he nodded. Rising from the chair, he made his way back to the counter and held out his hand for Jamie's coins. After comparing the coins in his hands to the pictures in his ledger, he nodded again.

"Yup, there's no doubt about it. These are the same coins."

"I knew it!" Jamie shouted, stuffing the coins in the front pocket of his jeans.

I glanced up at the owner to see his reaction, and sure enough, the man still looked confused. "Um, thank you so much for your time. We really do appreciate it."

Grabbing Jamie by the arm, I led him toward the front of the store where Scott and Phyllis were waiting. Giving them both a look which said, "Let's talk about it outside," I opened the door and stepped out into the afternoon sunlight.

# CHAPTER EIGHT

## Time To Kill

"Should we go see Mr. Reed again?" Phyllis asked after I had explained what the owner of *Checkered Past* had said about the coins. "We need to tell him what we found out."

"That's true," Scott said, "but Mr. Reed said he would be busy all afternoon with some research. Perhaps it would be better if we talked to him tomorrow."

"So what should we do in the meantime?" Jamie asked. "Should we go to the police?"

I stared up into the cloudless sky as we climbed on our bikes and weighed our options. We now had proof that Jamie's coins had been stolen, but was that enough to go to the police? As much as I wanted to catch the bad guys, I knew the best thing to do at this point was to wait for Mr. Reed to do his research and find out what he could about the counterfeit operation it seemed Mr. Oldie was running.

After stating my opinion to the others, I continued, "Besides Jamie's coins gave me an idea of some combinations we haven't tried yet. How about we go back to Pop-Pop's and see if we can open that secret compartment?"

"What about Watson?" Jamie cried.

"What about him?" I asked, turning back to look at my brother.

"You said we could take him to the park when we were done at the shops. You promised, Abby, and I already told him we were going to the park this afternoon. He'll be upset if we don't go."

I smiled. "You're right, Jamie. I forgot all about it. How about we take Watson for a quick trip to the park first, and then we'll go back to Pop-Pop's house and try out some of my ideas?

Everyone agreed, and we eagerly made our way back to the house.

---

"Jamie, we'll need some of those books on the Freemasons that you borrowed from the library," I said as we reached the top of the staircase. The stuffed owl hanging on the wall just above the steps used to give me the creeps, but now I found myself reaching out to pet it every time I went upstairs. I guess I got used to him.

"What do you need my books for?" Jamie asked. "And what do my coins have to do with your desk? You said my coins gave you an idea about the combination."

Hurrying past Jamie, I grabbed the books off his nightstand and headed into my adjoining bedroom. "We know that Nathanael Greene was a Freemason, just like your coins. There are dates on your coins, right?"

Jamie examined the two coins he had pulled from his pocket and nodded.

"Well, maybe one of those dates or another date that's important to the Freemasons is the combination to open the desk. It makes sense, don't you think?"

Scott and Phyllis nodded as they sat down on the bed. Jamie, holding the first coin close to his face, read off the three dates. "1976, 1735, 1776."

"The year 1976 wouldn't be it," Scott said, "because Greene was long dead by then."

"Right!" I cried, snapping my fingers. "So, we can try the other two, though I think we already tried 1776 because that was such an important date in history."

Setting the books on top of the desk, I bent down to open the first drawer but stopped when Jamie called my name.

"May I do it?" he asked. "That way you don't have to get down on the floor."

I appreciated the offer since I really wasn't interested in crawling around on the floor, so I nodded, and Jamie took his place under the desk. We started with the year 1735, and Jamie opened each door to the appropriate number starting with the lefthand drawer and working his way across. When that didn't work, he tried opening the big middle drawer at the top first and then the remaining drawers left to right. Nothing. After repeating the same process with the year 1776, we still hadn't discovered a secret compartment.

I let out a deep breath and grabbed the books from the top of the desk. "Well, I guess we'll need to dig a little deeper." After handing a book to Jamie, then Scott, and then Phyllis, I opened my emergency bag and pulled out a notepad and four pens. I gave everyone a sheet of paper and a pen and explained, "We're looking for any dates that are important to the Masons. Write down anything you find, and we'll try them when we're done."

Within just a couple of minutes, Phyllis spoke up, "Cool! This might be easier than I thought."

I glanced up to see what she was talking about. Turning her book my way, she commented, "This book has a chapter titled, *The Freemason Calendar.* There's a whole list of dates here and why they're important, like in 1706, Benjamin Franklin was born and in 1756, Mozart was born." Running her finger down the page, she skimmed the dates there. "There are a lot of dates for when certain lodges were established, whatever that means. . .oh, and here's the year George Washington was born."

I bounced up from the floor where I'd been sitting. "What was that?"

My sudden movement startled Phyllis, causing her to jump back. "George Washington was born in 1732," she mumbled.

"That's it!" I cried. "That has to be it!"

Scott tilted his head to one side. "Why does that have to be it? Why would Greene use George Washington's birthday?"

"They were best friends! In fact, Greene thought so much of Washington that he named his son George Washington and his daughter, Martha Washington. It makes sense to me that he would use his dear friend's birthday. Let's try it!"

Jamie dropped the book he'd been reading and scooted under the desk once more. First, he opened the left drawer until it reached the number one on the underside. Next, he opened the big middle drawer to the seven, then the small middle one to three, and finally, he pulled out the right and final drawer until it hit two. Nothing happened.

"I don't think that's it," Jamie said.

"Maybe not," I responded, praying that we hadn't reached another dead end. "But try opening the drawers in the other order."

Using the same year, Jamie open the drawers one at a time, this time beginning with the top drawer and then working the other drawers from left to right. As the right drawer reached the two, I heard a faint click and jumped back when a small panel opened up on the left side of the desk.

On the floor, Jamie looked as shocked as I felt. "It worked. There really is a secret compartment!"

As Jamie struggled to get out from under the desk, Scott, Phyllis and I moved closer to get a better look at the new opening. Prying the panel open a bit further with my fingers, I spied what appeared to be a book. Freeing it from its dark cocoon, I pulled the leather book to me and carefully flipped through the yellowed pages. I could feel my eyes widening as I stared at the treasure in my hands.

"It's a journal," I whispered. "Nathanael Greene's journal."

"Are you sure?" Scott asked, standing behind me and peering over my shoulder.

"I'm sure. Listen to this, *The Brits seem determined to steal our land and our freedom. Despite their numerous losses, they persevere. Not only are my men outnumbered, but most of them are farmers and shopkeepers – hardly soldiers of war. Still, it is our lot to keep the British from advancing farther north, and by God's grace, that is what we will do.*

"Wow!" Jamie exclaimed, then pointed at the next page. "What's that?"

Staring at the strange lines and figures, I shook my head, trying to make sense of what I was seeing. "My guess is it's some sort of code or secret writing. There are figures like that on many of these pages."

"Maybe it's a secret message about a treasure or something like that. I read that a lot of soldiers buried their money to keep it from the enemy, but many of them never had the chance to dig it up again. Maybe some of these messages are clues to buried fortunes," Jamie declared.

Running over to pick up one of the Freemason books off the floor, he flipped it open to a page that had similar looking numbers, letters and squiggles. "See, they're codes and ciphers. I bet if we use these books we can figure out what they say."

"Codes and secret messages," Phyllis declared. "I'm really starting to feel like a secret agent!"

I knew exactly how she felt.

# CHAPTER NINE
## The Surprises Keep Coming

After all the excitement of discovering the journal, the afternoon seemed to move by in slow motion. Though we spent most of the time reading through Greene's journal and decoding the many ciphers it contained, we were disappointed to find out that they were mostly military codes and battle plans that were no longer relevant. I, for one, was hoping to find clues about a lost treasure or some other big secret, but after reading through the journal, I realized that Nathanael Greene had serious financial issues. In fact, he died deeply in debt—most of which was not his fault.

It seems Greene's many troubles began when he was named quartermaster for the army during the war. The quartermaster was the one in charge of supplying food, clothing, weapons and more to all the soldiers. When Greene discovered there wasn't enough money to provide for all the soldiers' needs, he took out loans against his own property to ensure his men were well-fed and properly clothed. On top of this, Greene made some investments that went terribly wrong. But the biggest hit to his financial standing was when he cosigned[9] on a loan for a couple of fellow soldiers who refused to pay off the loan and ran away, leaving Greene to pay off the debt himself.

It was obvious from the journal that Greene was a proud man who did not feel right about being in debt. He spent the last several years of his life trying to pay off the debt but died before he had the chance. One of the last entries in his journal was this:

I have done everything in my power to make things right with my creditors, but I do not have the funds to appease their demands. I have but one last recourse, and I am too ashamed to speak of it further.

The four of us kids spent some time researching through the various library books we had to see if we could find out what Greene was talking about, but we didn't find anything. We did, however, uncover other interesting questions.

"Here's what I don't get," Jamie said as we gathered in the detective office. The downstairs room had once been a bedroom, but Pop-Pop converted it into an office for us after we solved our first big case. The small room consists of a desk, a couple of chairs, two narrow bookshelves, a giant bean bag and a large cork board that hangs on the wall behind the desk. The light-blocking curtains keep the room cool and dark, the perfect environment for solving mysteries. Jamie sprawled on the bean bag in the corner of the room.

"How could Nathanael Greene die so poor and in so much debt when he was awarded all that land and money for his years of service in the army? I mean, it says here that he received ten thousand gold coins from South Carolina and five thousand from Georgia. I don't know how much money gold coins were worth back then, but surely it would've been enough to pay off his debt."

"Not to mention the land," Phyllis chimed in. "He was awarded a timber plantation in North Carolina plus a plantation in South Carolina and another one in Georgia. And these weren't little properties either. There were thousands of acres.  If he had sold the properties, wouldn't that have been enough to settle his debts?"

"It's hard to say," Scott answered. "I guess it would depend on how much debt there was."

"It must've been a lot," I interrupted. "From everything we've read, it's obvious that Greene was a good, honest man and that he was very smart. I'm sure if he could've sold the lands and paid off his debts, he would have. Something tells me it wasn't quite as simple as all that."

"It's actually sad," Scott replied. "He gave so much for this country and then died in debt, so much so that his widow had to sell off all of his belongings, including his desk and bookshelf."

"So much for buried treasure," Jamie whined as he flopped backward on the bean bag.

We all sat quietly, lost in our thoughts. I couldn't help but wonder if Mrs. Greene knew about the journal. Surely if she had known, she would've kept it for herself. But then, if she had, I probably wouldn't have it now, so I guess it worked out pretty well for me.

---

After several minutes of gloomy thoughts, an idea struck me. "Oh, with everything else going on this afternoon, I nearly forgot. Scott and I need to tell you two what we overheard at *Oldie's* right before we left."

Jamie and Phyllis snapped to attention. Jamie slid to the edge of the bean bag, his hands resting on his knees while Phyllis sat at the desk in one of the swivel chairs. Despite their obvious interest in what I had to say, they both looked tired, and I wondered if we would be able to pull off the very thing I was about to explain to them.

Scott and I spent the next few minutes telling about the open door in the back corner of Oldie's store and how we had overheard the two men talking about an evening shipment. Our younger siblings agreed with us that the entire ordeal[10] sounded suspicious.

"So, what I'm suggesting is that we spy on the shipment tonight. If we can catch Mr. Oldie in the act of doing something wrong, then the police will have no choice but to arrest him."

"There's no way our mom will let us do that," Phyllis said. "We have to be in bed by ten."

"What time is the shipment supposed to take place anyway?" Jamie asked, pulling his knees to his chest.

Scott and I exchanged glances.

"We're not exactly sure," I said, "but we do know it will be after the store closes, which happens at eight o'clock."

"So, you want us to just sit outside watching the store from eight o'clock until whenever?" Jamie asked with a scowl.

"Do you have a better idea?" Scott replied, joining Jamie on the floor.

The room was quiet for several moments as everyone, once again, seemed lost in their own thoughts. I knew the idea was risky and that it would take some convincing for Pop-Pop to allow us to leave the house so late in the evening, but I felt sure that this secret shipment was the proof we'd been looking for. It was important that we be there to see what was going on.

Hugging his knees to his chest and rocking from side to side, Jamie finally spoke. "All right, I'm in, but you have to find a way to get us out of the house without lying to Pop-Pop."

"Deal," I agreed.

After we headed upstairs, I walked over to my desk and opened the top drawer. Placing the journal in the drawer, my fingernail caught on the back cover, and I heard a ripping sound. "Oh no!" I cried, pulling the book up to my face to see the damage. As I did, a piece of yellowed paper floated to the floor, landing inches from Jamie's foot.

"What in the world?" he asked, bending down and grabbing the page.

I scanned the journal and noticed that the back cover had pulled away from the leather binding. It was like there was a secret compartment within the journal itself. "What is it?" I asked Jamie as the others huddled around him, trying to see over his shoulder.

"It's a letter from some guy named Lafayette."

"The Marquis de Lafayette?" I asked excitedly.

Jamie shrugged. "I don't know. It's hard to read this fancy writing."

He handed the letter over to me, and I read it aloud.

*My Dearest Nathanael,*

*It pains me deeply to hear of your financial distress, but I am pleased that you have sought my aid. You gave me a chance when no one else would. I am who I am today because of your faith in me. I owe you a great debt and am honored at this opportunity to provide you with assistance. As it happens, I foresaw this catastrophe and made arrangements the last time we were together. Your salvation is nearer than you could possibly know. I have faith that you will review this offer and that your expectations of aid will be met in the pages to follow. Should you need more, you need only ask.*

*Your Loyal Friend,*
*Lafayette*

"What do you think it means?" Phyllis asked.

"I'd say this was the unspeakable thing that Greene talked about in his journal. It sounds to me like he asked this guy Lafayette for some money to help settle his debts," Scott replied.

"Well, Lafayette certainly had money to offer," I said. "He was a marquis, which is a position of high rank and wealth in France where he was from. He later lost his home and fortune and even wound up in prison for starting a freedom uprising in France, but before that, he was very wealthy. In fact, he used a lot of his money to help the American soldiers in the Revolutionary War. He was a war hero, just like Greene."

"So, what's the big deal?" Jamie asked, plopping down on my bed. "Why would Greene be upset about asking his friend for money?"

"Remember," I answered, "Nathanael Greene was very proud. He liked to solve his own problems, make his own way. It would have been very awkward to have to ask his friend for money. Plus, Greene had been Lafayette's commanding officer. It would be like the principal asking us for money. It's weird. I can't blame Greene for being uncomfortable in having to ask his friend for help."

"Well," Jamie replied, "you know what the Bible says about pride. It leads to destruction."

"That's true," Scott said, taking the letter from my hand, "but it seems like Greene worked it out in the end. After all, this letter is proof that he did finally ask for help."

"But did he get it?" I wondered aloud. "Greene died in debt, so if Lafayette sent him money, what happened to it?" Taking the letter back, I reread it. "The pages to follow. I wonder if Lafayette was going to send another letter, or if there's more than one page to this one." Going back over to the journal, I examined the binding, looking for any other secret panels or evidence of a second page to the Frenchman's letter. There was nothing.

"It looks like either Greene never received another letter or that he never received the money."

"Or he died before he could," I remarked. "This letter is dated April 1786. If Lafayette sent this from France, it would have probably taken a month or so to reach Greene, who died in June of 1786. Perhaps, he just didn't get the information in time."

"But you would think his wife would have taken the money so that she didn't have to lose her home and all her stuff," Phyllis said.

"I'm not sure his wife knew anything about this. After all, this letter was hidden in his journal. Perhaps Mr. Greene didn't want to get his wife's hopes up. Maybe he was going to surprise her."

"I don't know," Jamie said, "but for now, we need to get some dinner so that we can get ready to solve another mystery."

# CHAPTER TEN

## Spies in the Dark

As it happened, the town library was hosting a movie night that very evening. The four of us, with permission from Pop-Pop and Mrs. Hicks (Scott and Phyllis' mom), left Pop-Pop's house around seven o'clock and made our way to the library. The movie was scheduled to begin at 7:30, and our plan was to sneak out shortly after the movie began and hopefully sneak back in before the movie was over.

Twenty minutes after the movie had started, the four of us rose from our chairs in the back of the theater room, and slipped out the door. Though the sun was going down, the evening air was still hot and muggy, and by the time we reached *Oldie's*, my shirt clung to me as beads of sweat trickled down my back. We settled in behind some bushes across the street from the back of the store. We figured if this was some kind of secret shipment, they probably wouldn't do it in the main parking lot but rather near the back door. Laying our bikes on the ground beside us, we hunched down behind the shrubbery and peered at the back of the

I Once Was Lost                                                    81 building, lit only by a single streetlamp as the darkness of night fell.

We knelt there for what seemed like an eternity, and I found myself constantly checking my watch. At one point, I got a cramp in my foot that nearly caused me to cry out in pain, but I managed to muffle my complaints as I massaged the knotted area.

"Someone's coming," Scott said.

Releasing my foot, I resumed my position on my knees and glanced through the bushes. Sure enough, a large box truck pulled in and backed up to the building. The driver of the truck got out of the vehicle, slamming the door behind him, and headed up the ramp toward the single metal door on the back side of the building. At the same time, a small man climbed down out of the passenger seat and followed in the shadow of the truck driver. It was too dark to see either man clearly, but something about the small man was familiar. After pushing a round button on the side of the door, the two men waited, glancing around nervously.

Within seconds, the door opened, and from the light within, the two men immediately became visible. The truck driver was a large, grizzled[11] man with arms the size of my waist. His shabby clothing and dingy ball cap set him apart from the elegance of many of the items I knew to be within the shop. He looked like he belonged in a pool hall rather than an antique store. I recognized the small man immediately, as he was the same one Scott and I had seen talking with Mr. Oldie earlier in the day—Mustache Man, as we decided to call him. Since he was in on this secret delivery, I guess it only made sense that he was present. Within seconds of the door opening, both men stepped through, pulling the door closed behind them. Silence echoed through the air.

"Well that's just great," Jamie complained. "There's no way we can spy on them now. This has been a waste of time."

I had to admit it seemed like Jamie was right. When I'd come up with the idea about spying on the evening shipment, it never occurred to me that they would handle business inside the building. What were we supposed to do now?

"Let's just wait here a few more minutes," Scott said. "If there really is a shipment, they'll have to come back out to get something out of the truck. Let's stick around and see if we can't make this worth our while after all."

I glanced down at my watch again. It was 8:37. I knew that if we waited much longer, we would miss our opportunity to sneak back into the library before the movie was over, but Scott had a point. So, we waited, and fortunately our patience paid off.

Several moments later, the truck driver exited the building, followed by Mr. Oldie and Mustache Man who had arrived with the truck. The wiry man was rubbing his hands together like a child awaiting an ice cream cone. Mr. Oldie seemed less excited as he followed the driver to the back of the truck and stood quietly. The man opened the back door.

"Can you see what's inside?" Phyllis asked.

"Not from here," I confessed. "We need to get somewhere we can see what's happening."

Scanning our surroundings, we decided on an area that seemed likely to give us a better vantage point to see inside the truck. Sneaking across the way one at a time, we squatted down behind a brick wall. From this angle, the streetlight was between us and the truck, lighting the inside of the vehicle and making it easier for us to identify the items within.

"Would you like to see the newest of your one-of-a-kind items?" Mustache Man asked with an eerie[12] giggle.

One-of-a-kind items? That wasn't what I saw. From what I could see, the truck contained three large dressers that looked like they dated back to perhaps the early 1900s. The odd thing about the dressers was they were identical. It wasn't like they were a set with three pieces of different sizes, but they were alike in every single way.

"Do you see what I see?" Scott asked.

"Gotcha!" Jamie exclaimed.

# CHAPTER ELEVEN

## Proof at Last

The next morning, we met up at Mr. Reed's shop. As we entered the store, the first thing I noticed was how tired Mr. Reed looked as he hunched over a stack of open books on the counter. At the sound of the bell, he looked up and rubbed his eyes.

"Oh, good, I was hoping you'd be here today. I have much to tell you."

"We have a lot to tell you too," Jamie said as the four of us strode to the counter.

Before Mr. Reed could respond, we explained to him about the discovery of the journal and our spy mission from the night before. We gave him every detail about what we had heard and seen outside of *Oldie's Antiques*. In our excitement, the four of us talked over one another as we all tried to fill in bits and pieces of the story. When we finished, I stared at Mr. Reed, certain that he would be thrilled with our findings, but instead, the look on his face was one of disapproval.

"Your grandfather and your parents gave you permission to go on such a spy mission alone?"

I grimaced. "Not exactly, but we did have permission to be out that late at night."

Mr. Reed folded his arms across his chest and tilted his head to one side. "And how is that exactly? What reason could you kids possibly have to be out that late at night?"

Before I could answer, Jamie spoke up. "Well, you see, the library was having a movie night, so we told Pop-Pop and Mrs. Hicks that that's where we were going."

"You mean you lied?" Mr. Reed asked.

I shifted my weight from one foot to another, suddenly uneasy with the direction the conversation had turned. As I was trying to come up with something to say, Scott—who was also swaying on his feet—decided to speak up.

"We didn't exactly lie. We did go to the movie night at the library. We just left after it started, but we were there for some of it. So, it wasn't really a lie. We went where we said we were going to go."

I shook my head, knowing this was not going to end well.

Mr. Reed uncrossed his arms and laid his hands, palm down, on the counter, leaning forward to the point where his face was only inches from ours. "Oh, I see. So, because part of your story was true, it doesn't matter that you left out the rest of it? I would have thought you would have learned that lesson from the story of the Resolute desks."

Scott didn't respond, and it was clear to me he regretted speaking up in the first place. The four of us stood quietly, waiting to hear what Mr. Reed would say next.

The store owner shook his head. "What you kids did was very dangerous, but more than that, it was wrong. I don't care how you look at it or how much you sugarcoat it, when you don't tell the whole truth, it's still a lie. It doesn't matter if you tell half the truth or even most of the truth, if you leave out or change any part of it, it's a lie, and I think, deep down, you kids know that. If you didn't, you would be defending yourselves right now instead of standing there in shame. You owe your grandfather and your parents an apology and an explanation of what you were really doing last night. It's up to them how they want to proceed from there, but I don't mind telling you that I'm disappointed. I expected more from you."

Tears sprang to my eyes. I don't know what was worse: Mr. Reed's lecture or the fact that he was disappointed in us. Over the past few weeks, we'd grown to really like and respect the elderly man. To know that he thought less of us at this point was truly heartbreaking. But he was right. We did know better. At least, I did. I understand—and have understood for a while now—that telling a half-truth is the same as telling a whole lie. But I knew that Pop-Pop would have never let us go if I told him the truth, so I convinced myself that it was worth a little lie to get what I wanted. But now, I realize that I was lying to myself as much as I was lying to Pop-Pop. Lying is never worth it, and it only brings trouble.

Mr. Reed spoke again, interrupting my thoughts. "Probably the worst part about the whole thing is that you kids risked your lives for nothing. I understand you saw something, but at this point, it's your word against his, and that's not really proof, is it?"

The four of us shook our heads, realizing—it seems, for the first time—that Mr. Reed had a point. It didn't matter what we heard or saw because we had no proof.

"Fortunately," Mr. Reed continued, "I have found proof. Mr. Oldie is definitely selling counterfeit antiques." The store owner grabbed the book that was lying open on top of the stack in front of him, and turned it in our direction, pointing to a picture on the left-hand page. "See this painting here? Do you recognize it?"

I couldn't be sure, but I thought it looked like one I remembered seeing at Mr. Oldie's store.

"It says here that this painting is currently hanging in a museum in Philadelphia. I called the museum last night to be certain, and sure enough, the painting is there. However, I saw the same painting at *Oldie's Antiques* yesterday."

"How can you be sure that the one in Oldie's store is the counterfeit and not the one in the museum?" Phyllis asked, surprising all of us with such an intelligent question.

Mr. Reed nodded and waved his hand over the open books in front of him. "Because that isn't the only item that is not authentic." Grabbing another book from the pile, he turned it our way. "This chair here is part of a collection put together by Ronald Reagan when he was president. According to my sources, when Reagan left the White House, the collection remained to be enjoyed by all those who were to follow after him. It took many tries, but I finally was able to get hold of the White House secretary late last night, who confirmed that the chair is still in one of the rooms of the White House."

"And I take it there is no chance that there were two chairs that were identical?" I asked, making sure I understood what Mr. Reed was trying to say.

"From what I could find through my research, there was only the one chair." Again, Mr. Reed gestured to the open books on the counter. "All of these books contain items that I saw at Oldie's store that are reported to be displayed elsewhere. There are simply too many accounts for it to be a coincidence. And based on what you kids saw last night, I think it's safe to say that Mr. Oldie is a crook."

"Well, what are we waiting for?" Jamie asked, slamming his fist into the palm of his opposite hand. "Let's go tell the police."

Mr. Reed frowned and shook his head again. "I'm afraid there's more, and I'm almost too ashamed to tell you." Shuffling through the books on the counter, he glanced at each one until he came to a small blue book which he lifted and turned toward us. Pointing at the picture in the bottom right corner, he continued. "Take a good look at this Scrimshaw."

"What's a Scrimshaw?" Scott asked.

A small smile crossed Mr. Reed's face. "It is a carving done on bone, ivory, or whale's teeth. Most of them date back to the 1800s and are worth quite a bit of money. This brooch, for example, is worth over six thousand dollars."

I stared at the picture of the lovely pin engraved with the seashore, a lighthouse and a bird in flight. It was a peaceful scene and made me long for another trip to the beach before we headed back to our home in South Carolina.

"This piece is now in the personal collection of some rich family in New York. As with the other items, I made calls last night to validate this. Now look," Mr. Reed said, pushing the book aside and clearing an empty space on the glass countertop. Following his pointed finger, I looked down into the glass case and gasped. The exact same brooch sat nestled in a bed of felt inside the case.

"But how?" I asked, turning my eyes toward Mr. Reed. "You're not a thief. How can you possibly have this?"

Mr. Reed ran his hand through his hair and blew out a deep breath. "It would seem, my dear, that I've been duped.[13] It's not uncommon for an antique dealer to occasionally be sold counterfeit goods, but in my forty years of business, this is the first time it's happened to me. I'm so embarrassed."

Jamie placed his hand on top of Mr. Reed's. "It's not your fault. You didn't know."

Mr. Reed began to pace the floor, shaking his head and muttering, "No, I didn't know, but I should've been more careful. I should've done more research. I should have studied it out further before committing to buy it."

"Everyone makes mistakes," Scott said in a quiet and friendly tone.

An odd thought struck me. "Just out of curiosity, where did you get it from?"

The shop owner stopped pacing and turned to face me. "That's the worst part. It was one of my usual suppliers. I've gotten items from him for probably close to ten years. I can only hope that he wasn't aware that it was a counterfeit either, but I guess I'll find out soon enough. I called him first thing this morning, and he's on his way over. Before I do anything else, I've got to get to the bottom of this."

As if on cue, the door swung open, ringing the bell over the doorway, and we all turned in its direction. There was a collective gasp in the air as the four of us recognized Mustache Man. The man looked at us and smiled a creepy grin, then turned to Mr. Reed.

"I came as soon as I could," he said to the storeowner. "So, what's this emergency you called about?"

I couldn't believe my ears. Mr. Reed's supplier was the same one we saw with Mr. Oldie? How could that be? I felt the need to warn him, but I didn't know any way to let him know about his guest without alerting the man to our knowledge of his illegal activities the night before.

"Why don't you kids come back at lunch time?" Mr. Reed said. "Once I get to the bottom of this, we'll know how to proceed."

The four of us exchanged glances, and I could tell by the uneasiness in their eyes, that each of the others agreed with me that we should warn Mr. Reed about his supplier, but the two men had already made their way to the back office and closed the door. For the time being, we had to accept that Mr. Reed was alone with the enemy.

# CHAPTER TWELVE
## Help!

"What should we do now?" Phyllis asked as the four of us huddled outside Mr. Reed's shop.

Scott looked over his shoulder as if to make sure we weren't being watched or overheard. "I think we should go to the police. We have enough proof now that they should be able to make a case against Mr. Oldie and Mustache Man."

"I agree," I said. "Besides, I'm afraid Mr. Reed might be in danger. We need to get help, and we need to get it fast."

Even on our bicycles, the trip to the police station took far longer than I would've hoped, and with every passing moment, I was terrified for Mr. Reed. What if Mustache Man grew suspicious of Mr. Reed's intentions? What if he attacked the elderly man? As we've seen with criminals in the past, there's just no telling what they might do. If they're willing to break one law, chances are they have no problem breaking another. The more I thought about it, the faster my legs pedaled.

When we finally arrived at the police station, I was out of breath, but that didn't stop me from hopping off my bicycle and running through the front door—Jamie and our two friends following close behind me. Typically, I would ask the officer at the front counter if Detective Lawrence was in. He was a friend of ours and had helped us in some of our past cases. But this was not a typical situation, and I was frantic[14] with worry for Mr. Reed, so as soon as I reached the front counter, I spilled out our entire tale. My voice was loud even to my own ears, and I was having trouble holding back the tears as I tried to explain the situation. I could tell from the look on the officer's face that he couldn't understand me, and if anything, he seemed uncomfortable with my tears.

The commotion in the front of the station brought officers out of many of the other rooms. Detective Lawrence was among them, and as soon as he saw us, he ushered us into his office. After closing the door behind him and dropping down into his chair, he said, "Okay, now, what's this all about?"

He was looking at me, but Scott spoke up. "We need to report a crime of counterfeit and also another crime that may be happening at this very moment." Scott went on to calmly explain everything that we had learned about Mr. Oldie and Mustache Man, including the fact that the latter was meeting with Mr. Reed at that very moment. Scott detailed how Mr. Reed had found out that he had been a victim of a counterfeit operation but how we were certain the elderly shop owner had no idea that he was selling counterfeit goods. The more Scott revealed, the more Detective Lawrence leaned in his chair, stretching so far forward that I feared he may fall on the floor.

As Scott neared the end of the story, Jamie spoke up. "Please, Mr. Reed could be in danger. Could you send some officers over there?"

"From what you kids have told me, the situation does sound serious. I'll round up another detective and we'll head over there right away. I'll need one of you kids to ride with us to identify this man you call Mustache Man. The rest of you can stay here at the station."

The four of us exchanged glances, each knowing that we all secretly wanted to go yet not wanting to take too long to decide.

"Abby, why don't you go?" Scott said. "You know the most about the situation, and you'll easily be able to recognize Mustache Man. We'll wait here for you."

I studied the faces of Jamie and Phyllis as they nodded in agreement. Accepting their decision, I followed Detective Lawrence out of his office and down the narrow hallway where we met up with another officer who Detective Lawrence introduced as

Detective O'Reilly. Within a few minutes, we were in the police car and headed toward Mr. Reed's shop. The officers had decided to leave the lights and sirens off so as not to give away the element of surprise. They hoped to be able to sneak into the antique shop and arrest Mustache Man before he had the chance to do any harm. I prayed the whole way, asking God to protect Mr. Reed and to allow the police to arrest the bad guys.

When we arrived, Detective O'Reilly made it clear that I was to stay in the car. I didn't argue. For once, I wasn't sure I wanted to know what was going on behind closed doors. I watched from the car as the two men, their guns drawn, slipped into the building. Seconds later, they exited the shop, followed by Mr. Reed who closed the door, locked it and flipped the outside sign to where it read *Closed*. He and the officers joined me in the car, and we drove off in the direction of the police station.

"What happened?" I asked Mr. Reed as he crawled in to sit beside me in the backseat of the police car.

"I was about to ask you the same thing. Why are the police taking me in for questioning? I assume this has something to do with the counterfeit antiques, but I don't understand why you kids didn't wait for me. After all, I'm the one who has the proof."

I spent the drive back to the police station explaining to Mr. Reed about Mustache Man (whose name is actually Mr. Bennett, according to Mr. Reed). I told him how we feared for his safety and that we felt it was best if we went ahead and told the police what we knew. "Even if we didn't have enough proof for them to arrest anyone, we wanted to make sure that someone was there to see that nothing bad happened to you."

Mr. Reed's eyes filled with tears. "You kids are really something. It's been a long time since anyone cared enough about me to go through so much trouble to make sure I was safe. I don't know what to say."

"Say that you'll testify against Mr. Bennett and Mr. Oldie. They need to be behind bars."

Mr. Reed smiled. "That I can do. I'll give the police all the information I have about the counterfeit operation, including my own involuntary[15] involvement. Who knows? Maybe something good can come from all of this."

I smiled back at Mr. Reed and nodded. "I'm sure it will. After all, the Bible says, *All things work together for good to them who love God, to them who are the called according to his purpose.* I know I love God, and I believe you do too. This will all work out. You'll see."

# CHAPTER THIRTEEN

## The Long Afternoon

We spent the next couple of hours sitting in the police station. Detective Lawrence asked us to wait in the lobby while he questioned Mr. Reed. At one point, Detective O'Reilly drove Mr. Reed back to his shop so that he could gather up the evidence he had against Mr. Oldie and Mr. Bennett. We asked to tag along, but once again, Detective Lawrence instructed us to stay put. After sitting on the hard bench for over an hour, I began pacing the floor, growing more restless by the moment.

"I wish I had brought Greene's journal with me."

"Why?" Jamie asked. "What good would that do?"

"I'd have something to do. I'm bored just waiting here."

"We're all bored," Phyllis whined as she stretched her neck to one side then the other.

Finally, Detective Lawrence and Mr. Reed exited the office and came toward us down the narrow hallway. The shop owner looked relieved while the police officer seemed determine. There was a lot of whispering as the two men reached the front desk, along with a lot of letters and numbers which I can only assume were police codes. From their secret behavior, I had my doubts that we were going to find out any more information about this case. Yes, it seemed that our work was done.

As if reading my thoughts, Detective Lawrence came over to us. "You kids did a great job. We're heading over to *Oldie's Antiques* right now to bring him in for questioning. I need you kids to go home. We appreciate all your help, but we can take it from here."

He stared at each of us in turn as if making sure we understood his orders. I understood them just fine, but that didn't mean that I was happy about it. After saying "goodbye" to Mr. Reed, the four of us left the police station and moped our way to our bicycles parked nearby.

"That's the worst part about the detective business," Jamie said, kicking a small rock across the path in front of him. "We do all the work, but someone else gets all the credit. It's just not fair."

I knew exactly what Jamie was saying. It felt good to be a part of getting bad guys behind bars, but it was frustrating to do all the detective work only to be told that we couldn't follow through to see the end result.

"We could ride over to *Oldie's* and see what's happening," Phyllis offered. "We don't have to go in. We could watch from the park across the street like we did the other night. The police will never know we were there."

"But Detective Lawrence told us to go home," Scott replied. "We don't want to disobey a direct order."

I noticed a twinkle in my brother's eye. "What if we go home, then turn around and head over to *Oldie's*? We obeyed Detective Lawrence by going home, but he never said we had to stay there."

I shook my head. "No, Jamie. You and I both know that that wouldn't be right. It's just like Mr. Reed was talking about earlier—a half truth is a whole lie. We know that when Detective Lawrence told us to go home, he meant for us to stay away from *Oldie's*. If we go, we'd be disobeying."

Jamie sighed and hung his head. "You're right, Abby. I don't know what I was thinking."

"So, I guess we'd better head on back to Pop-Pop's," I shrugged. "Watson could probably use the company."

As we reached our neighborhood, we spotted Mrs. Hicks in her front yard. She waved us over.

"Scott. Phyllis. I'm glad you're home. I just found out that your grandmother is coming to spend the weekend with us, and there are a million things to do before she gets here. I need to run to the grocery store, and while I do that, I need the two of you to work on cleaning the house." She placed one hand on her hip and pointed at the siblings with a finger from the other hand. "I suggest you start with your bedrooms."

The brother and sister looked embarrassed. "Yes, ma'am."

After putting the bikes away in their garage, we parted ways. Scott and Phyllis went inside to complete their chores while Jamie and I headed over to Pop-Pop's house, uncertain how we would spend the afternoon. Once inside, we greeted Watson who was wound up from being closed in the laundry room all day.

"Why don't you take him outside for a little while?" I suggested. "It's not too hot out there today, and he could certainly use the exercise."

Jamie's face brightened. "I could train him some more. I know he could be a great watch dog. Let me get my stuff."

By "stuff," I knew he meant the ridiculous costume he wore while training Watson. The fact was that I wasn't sure Watson had it in him to be mean and ferocious, but at this point in time, it was making Jamie happy to believe it was possible, so who was I to burst his bubble?

After they went outside, I had the house to myself. There was really only one thing that sounded appealing, so I made my way up the stairs and into my room. Flopping down on my bed, I pulled Greene's journal out from the nightstand drawer and opened it to the page I had earmarked. Propping up on my pillow, I made myself comfortable and began to read. Before long, I found the answer to one of the questions we had been asking—what happened to the money and land Greene was awarded?

------------------◆------------------

It seems that Greene led a very difficult life, and things were never easy for him. Though already deeply in debt by the end of the war, the Revolutionary War general was certain that he could turn things around. He spent the money he was awarded to buy slaves to work his land so that he could make enough money from the land to pay off his debts. Even though he was against slavery, he felt it was the only way he could profit from the land. He had to have workers, and he couldn't afford to pay the average man's salary, so slaves seemed to be the only answer. Greene felt he was sitting on a gold mine if he could only get the land ready for harvest. In a letter to his friend Lafayette, he wrote, "This Country affords a fine field for making a fortune." Sadly, Greene had no idea what tragedies were awaiting him.

In 1784, a hurricane destroyed half of all Greene's crops. Then, in 1786, he lost fifty barrels of rice in a fire, and only a short time later, forty-five barrels sank in an accident on the Savannah River. A few years before that, wet weather and late planting destroyed much of his South Carolina crop. It seemed like no matter how hard he tried or how much he worked, he was destined to remain in debt. I found myself nearly in tears as I read his emotional account. "My heart is too full and my situation too distressing to write much... My situation is truly afflicting! To be reduced from independence to want, and from the power of obliging my friends, to a situation claiming their aid... My heart faints within me when I think of my family."

It was all too sad. No wonder he had died in debt. No wonder all his money was gone and his lands were nothing. I thought back to the verse I had quoted to Mr. Reed just a few hours before, and I began to pray. "God, your Word says that you work all things for our good if we love you and are saved. Based on everything I've read about Nathanael Greene, I'm pretty sure he was saved, but it doesn't seem like all things worked out for him. In fact, it seems like nothing worked out. He died in debt. His family was left with nothing. He risked his life over and over again for his country, yet it seemed like it was all for nothing. I know your word is true, Lord, but I'm afraid I don't understand this. Please help me to understand."

Deep in thought, I moved from my bed to the window and glanced out to the backyard. Despite the confusion and sympathy swelling within me, I couldn't help but smile. Jamie, dressed in his "training gear," motioned for Watson, who was content to chase a butterfly then flop down on the grass and do what we like to call "the doggie dance." That's where a dog lies on his back with his feet straight up in the air and twists his head and tail one way and then another. Watson was a good "dancer," but I don't think Jamie was impressed at this point in time.

I opened my window using the old crank at the base of the glass and leaned out to hear what Jamie was saying. He walked over to Watson and rubbed his belly. The dog's tongue lolled[16] to one side as Jamie spoke.

"Come on, boy, I need you to do this for me. You don't want the bad guys to hurt me, do you?"

I couldn't be certain because I was quite a distance from my brother, but I thought I heard a catch in his voice, like maybe he was about to cry. Jamie was a lot of things, but he wasn't a crier. For the first time that day, I realized that he might be glad that Detective Lawrence wouldn't allow us to tag along. It seemed my younger brother was a lot more fearful than I knew.

Before I could think more on that, I heard the door open downstairs and Pop-Pop calling our names.

# CHAPTER FOURTEEN
## Pop-Pop To The Rescue

I met our grandfather at the bottom of the stairs, and obviously, the look on my face told him that I was upset.

"What's the matter?" he asked. "Is something wrong? Where's your brother?"

As we settled down in the living room, I explained to him about the events of the morning and how, after helping the police, we were sent on our way. I described how frustrated we all felt being left out of the final stages of the investigation, but Pop-Pop only nodded.

"It's probably for the best," he said. "Detective Lawrence was right to send you kids home and keep you safe from harm, though I can see how it would make you feel angry and left out."

We sat in silence for a few moments, then Jamie joined us, Watson bounding at his heels. "This dog is not as smart as we thought he was. He refuses to learn even the simplest of tricks. I really thought he was smarter than that." With that exclamation, Jamie flopped down beside me on the couch and huffed loudly.

The room was silent except for Watson's tail thumping against the hardwood floor. For once in my life, I felt like I didn't have anything to say. Fortunately, I didn't have to say anything.

Pop-Pop stretched and stood from his recliner. "Well, I don't know about you kids, but I'm starving. How about we go over to Dunn and eat at that little deli? You know, the one that has the outside eating area."

My eyes opened wide. "You mean the one across from *Oldie's Antiques*?"

Pop-Pop smiled slightly then straightened his features as if to cover his humor. "Yes, now that I think about it, it is across from *Oldie's Antiques*."

At this turn in the conversation, Jamie sat up and leaned forward, resting his weight on his knees. "You mean we can go? But what about what Detective Lawrence said?"

"Detective Lawrence told you kids to go home, and you did that. And beyond that, you stayed home instead of sneaking back out. I'm proud of you for that. But the way I see it, we're not going to *Oldie's Antiques*. We're

I Once Was Lost

going to the deli across the street. Furthermore, you're not going alone; I'm going with you. Besides, from what you told me, I would imagine all of the excitement a t *Oldie's* is over now. The police have had several hours to deal with Mr. Oldie and to do whatever they needed to do around his store. Chances are, there won't be anything to see by the time we get there, but I figured it might give you kids some closure[17] to at least have a look."

Jumping up from the couch, I ran over to Pop-Pop and wrapped my arms around his waist. "You are the best grandfather ever!"

Pop-Pop laughed and hugged me in return. "Well, if we're going to go, we need to get going. Like I said, I'm starving!"

We were out the door in just a few minutes, and not long after that, we seated ourselves at a round table outside of the little deli. Since there was an outside dining area, the restaurant allowed dogs, so we were able to take Watson with us. With his leash latched securely to his neck, he hunkered[18] down under the table, enjoying some of the breadcrumbs that Jamie tossed his way. We had invited Scott and Phyllis to join us as well, but Mrs. Hicks had them busy getting the house ready for their grandmother who was coming to stay with them for a while.

From where we sat, we had an unobstructed[19] view of *Oldie's Antiques*. Just as Pop-Pop had suspected, the place was quiet, and there was no sign of police or anything else out of the ordinary. Still, there was a sense of peace in returning to the scene of the crime, as it were. Closure, as Pop-Pop had called it.

"May we walk over there after dinner?" Jamie asked, sipping on his tea. "We don't have to go inside or anything. I just want to look around for a minute."

Pop-Pop seemed uncertain. Glancing over at the antique store, he studied the surroundings. Seemingly satisfied that there was no danger, he nodded his head. "I don't see any harm in it, but we'll stick together. Is that understood?"

"Yes sir," we both replied.

We ate our meal mostly in silence, our attention repeatedly drawn to the building across the street. When we finished eating, Pop-Pop paid the bill, and after gathering our things, we made our way over to *Oldie's Antiques*. The building looked as it always had with one exception—the "Open" light on the front door was off, signifying the store was closed.

"Huh," Jamie grunted, "the store's not supposed to close until eight o'clock."

"Well, with all that's happened today, I'm sure they had no choice but to close the store." Pop-Pop continued, "After all, who would run it if Mr. Oldie has been arrested?"

Suddenly I heard a noise, like a squeaky door. I looked around but didn't see anything except for Watson who had pulled his ears back like he does when he's heard a sound that he can't identify. Realizing that we were standing on a busy street, I chided myself for being so suspicious about a squeaking sound. Little did I know that my instincts were serving me well at that moment.

As we made our way back to Pop-Pop's truck, a slight movement to my right caught my attention, and I turned to see a man sneaking through the alley behind the antique store. As if sensing my stare, the man looked up, and our eyes met.

"It's Mustache Man!" I shouted, pointing in the direction of the man who had somehow escaped the police.

The man turned and ran the opposite direction.

Before I knew what was happening, Watson had taken off, snatching the leash out of Jamie's hand. Within seconds, he had reached Mr. Bennett. Jumping into the air, Watson landed on the man's back, knocking him to the ground with a grunt. The ferocious dog stood with his front paws on Mr. Bennett's back, his teeth only inches from the man's neck, and the most hideous growl coming from his throat.

For a few moments, the three of us stood motionless, uncertain what to do. Once we regained our senses, we ran to where Watson was holding the man prisoner. Mustache Man was whimpering in pain, but he held perfectly still, obviously fearful of Watson's sharp teeth.

"Get him off me," he cried.

Pop-Pop shook his head, obviously still amazed at Watson's behavior. "I think we'll leave him right there until the police can get here. I believe they have a few questions for you."

Pop-Pop and Jamie remained there with Watson and Mr. Bennett while I ran back over to the deli to call the police, who arrived in less than ten minutes. When Detective Lawrence stepped out of his police car, he stared at the scene before him and scratched his head. "Well, there's something you don't see every day!"

With the police there, Jamie called Watson to his side. The dog, as if realizing the situation was under control, happily obeyed. At one moment, he appeared to be some ruthless, wild wolf-dog, but the next moment, he was his silly, playful self, bouncing in circles and rolling around on the ground. It was like the canine version of Dr. Jekyll and Mr. Hyde.[20]

"Good boy, Watson," Pop-Pop said. Then turning to Jamie he went on, "It looks like your training was successful after all."

Jamie only smiled and patted Watson's head, but I could tell he was very proud of the dog and maybe a little of himself, but I didn't really blame him for that. If it hadn't been for Watson, Mr. Bennett might have gotten away. This time, it was Watson who saved the day.

After arresting Mustache Man and placing him in the back of the police car, Detective Lawrence turned to Pop-Pop. "Would you mind following us to the police station? I'll need you to fill out a statement of what happened."

"We'd be happy to," Pop-Pop said.

We spent nearly two hours at the police station while Pop-Pop filled out a report, and each of us was questioned about what we saw. While there, we found out that Mr. Oldie had, indeed, been arrested for counterfeiting, and from the sound of it, Mr. Bennett would soon be joining him. There was an antique expert coming out within the week to go through everything in Oldie's store to sort out what was real and what wasn't.

"I'm afraid there's no reward this time, kids, but we really do appreciate your hard work," Detective Lawrence said with a smile.

I shrugged. "That's okay. We don't need a reward. Just knowing that there are two less bad guys loose in the world is enough reward for us."

Jamie rolled his eyes. "That sounds like a line from some cheesy detective novel."

"How would you know? You don't read!"

For a moment, a look of hurt crossed Jamie's face, but just as quickly as it came, it disappeared, and he started laughing.

"What's so funny?" I demanded, certain he was making fun of me.

Jamie held his stomach and tried to control his giggles. "I don't know. I guess this has just been a very strange day."

Well, that was one way to put it.

Detective Lawrence laughed along with Jamie, though I still couldn't figure out what was so funny. "As I said, there is no reward, but Jamie, I believe this belongs to you." Reaching into a brown envelope, the officer pulled out a stack of dollar bills. "Mr. Oldie has admitted to stealing your coins from your sister's bag on the first day you visited the shop. Since you had to buy them twice, I think it's only fair that you have this." Licking his thumb, Detective Lawrence counted out the bills and handed Jamie forty dollars.

"Thanks," Jamie said, taking the money and shoving it into the front pocket of his jeans. "I guess you were right, Abby. All things do work together for the good of those who love God."

His comment made me smile, but it also brought to memory my confusion over Nathanael Greene. Did God always keep His promises? Things certainly didn't seem to work out well for Greene.

# CHAPTER FIFTEEN

## Unbelievable!

As we made our way to Pop-Pop's truck, my grandfather seemed to sense my confusion, or at the very least, noticed the strange expression on my face.

"Abby, what's the matter? It's over. The bad guys are behind bars, and everyone is safe and sound. I thought you would be relieved."

Climbing into the passenger seat and settling my emergency bag between my feet, I buckled my seatbelt and turned to face Pop-Pop. "Oh, I am very relieved. It's good to know that Mr. Oldie and Mr. Bennett won't be tricking people anymore. It's just that I've been reading a lot in Nathanael Greene's journal, and there's a thought that's really been bothering me."

I went on to explain to Pop-Pop my thoughts about Romans 8:28, and how I knew that God promised that all things would work out for good to those who loved him. "But what about Nathanael Greene? I can tell from his writings that he loved God, but things certainly did not work out well for him. So what does that mean, Pop-Pop? I know God doesn't lie, but it seems like, in this case, he didn't keep his promise." I shook my head, weary from trying to make sense of it all. "I just don't know how to figure it out."

Pop-Pop was quiet for a moment as he focused on the road before him. Finally, he spoke. "I can understand your confusion, but sweetie, there's something you have to realize, and that's the fact that we won't always understand God's ways. You say that things didn't work out well for Nathanael Greene, but you don't know that. That's the way it looks to you, but you have to keep in mind that you don't have all the facts, and you don't see the whole picture. God does. He knows what He's doing, and He will always keep His word, even when it seems that He's not. It's difficult to understand and even more difficult to try to explain, so it's best if you just decide in your heart right now that God is always good and that He always keeps His promises. If you believe that and remember it even when things don't seem to be working out the way you think they should, you'll be able to get through, and you'll please God in the process."

Pop-Pop was right. Even though it was difficult to understand and even though it seemed like things didn't work out the way they should have, I needed to trust God. After all, faith is believing in things that you don't see or understand, not believing in the things that are right in front of you. I knew that God's word was true, so it was about time I started acting like it.

When we arrived at Pop-Pop's house, we discovered a message from Mr. Reed on the answering machine. He was excited and talking so quickly that we barely understood what he said. After listening to it a second time, we finally got the gist[21] of it. He said he had some really great news that he couldn't wait to share with us but he didn't want to share it over the phone, so he wondered if we could meet him at his shop at lunch time the next day. We tried returning the call to let him know that we had gotten his message and that we would be happy to meet him, but there was no answer on the other end. Evidently, he was not at the shop, and we didn't have his home number. So, we had no choice but to wait until the next day to find out what had him so excited.

Fortunately, Scott and Phyllis were able to join us the following day, and after an early lunch, the four of us made our way down to *Reed's Antiques*. Pop-Pop wanted to join us, but he needed to return to work. As for Watson, it seemed that his heroics from the night before had drained him of energy, and he seemed content to sleep the day away.

As we hurried to Mr. Reed's shop, the four of us took turns guessing what the news could be. Our guesses ranged from amusing to very far-fetched, but little did we know, the surprise was far better than we could have ever imagined and would unlock another mystery for us to solve.

As we entered the shop, Mr. Reed was with a customer, so we waited patiently, browsing the aisles. Well, when I say we waited patiently, I mean we tried to, but I honestly felt like I was about to vibrate out of my shoes. I love surprises, and since Mr. Reed works with antiques, I was secretly hoping that the surprise he had for us was something old and unique. According to the clock on the wall, only a few moments had passed, but it seemed like an eternity to me. Finally, the customer left, and Mr. Reed turned his attention to us. The smile on his face was so huge that it caused his eyes to squeeze shut.

"Come with me to the back room," he said, waving us toward the doorway in the rear of the shop. "I have something to show you."

We wasted no time as we followed Mr. Reed through the doorway and into the storeroom. The space consisted of a variety of shelves, each filled with antiques that, I assumed, were waiting to be repaired, studied, or logged before joining the others in the showroom. There were also a variety of tools and cleaning supplies presumably used for cleaning the antiques and making them presentable before putting them up for sale. In the middle of the room stood what I could only guess was a large piece of furniture covered by a tan sheet. Glancing around the room, I saw many interesting things but nothing that could warrant the excitement that Mr. Reed displayed.

Walking to the center of the room, Mr. Reed stopped before the covered piece of furniture and grabbed the edge of the tan sheet, whipping it off in a single, fluid motion. My jaw dropped to the floor, and I could not believe my eyes.

"You found the bookcase!" Jamie exclaimed.

Mr. Reed nodded. I stared at the sight before me, trying to wrap my brain around the fact that I was looking at the matching bookcase to Nathanael Greene's campaign desk – the one sitting in my bedroom at Pop-Pop's house. The bookcase was made of the same wood and possessed many of the same lines and symbols as the desk. The case had four thick shelves—divided in half by another solid piece of wood — and at the bottom, there were three large cabinets concealed by doors. The doors were decorated with the most unusual emblems, and I wondered if there was any significance to them, like if they were perhaps some form of Masonic symbol. Each door had a wide trim, and in the center, there was something resembling a shield, on top of which was—well—a wooden egg, at least that's what it reminded me of. But the wood of the egg itself was carved with little round notches, giving it the appearance of dragon skin. It was kind of cool. Big swirly leaves stretched out from both sides of the shield. Even though these particular emblems weren't on the desk, there was still no doubt that this was the matching bookcase. The style and other lines were too similar. Sadly, it was in rough shape. The wood had been blackened and even charred in several areas, and many of the shelves were scratched, but I didn't care. It was still beautiful to me.

"How did you find it?" I asked, turning my attention to the store owner.

Mr. Reed laughed and clapped his hands together in excitement. "It was the strangest thing. As you know, I've been searching for the bookcase ever since I purchased the desk. I had hoped to sell the two as a set, but when you bought the desk, I continued to search for the bookcase anyway. I had called every dealer I could think of, and no one had any idea where the bookcase could be. It seemed like it had vanished from off the face of the earth, and to be honest, I had given up hope of ever finding it. Then, the other night when I was calling around to get information about the counterfeits I had found at *Oldie's*, I came upon a lead—a dealer who said that he had sold the bookcase to a local church several years ago. I didn't say anything to you kids because I knew it was a long shot, but yesterday, when all the mess with the police was over, I called the church and found out that they did, in fact, have the bookcase. They told me that it had been in their possession for quite some time and that it had burned in a fire in one of their downstairs rooms shortly after they purchased the bookcase. Since then, they've kept it but haven't really used it. When I explained who I was and why I wanted it, they offered to give it to me if I could go and get it. So, that's what I did. I had my guys pick it up this morning, then I cleaned it up a little bit, and here it is."

As he talked, Mr. Reed walked around the bookcase, sliding his hand up and down the wood and examining the burn marks. When he was finished, however, he turned toward us. "And I want you kids to have it."

"What?" the four of us asked in unison.

Shoving his hands into his pockets, Mr. Reed looked to the floor and then back at us. "I owe you kids big time! If it hadn't been for you, I could be selling counterfeit goods right now without even knowing it. If I had done that and been caught, I could've lost my business license and even my freedom. You kids saved me from all that, so giving you this bookcase is the least I can do. After all, you already have the desk, so you might as well keep the set together."

I couldn't believe it. My heart was beating so fast that I felt like it was going to pop right out of my chest. Following Mr. Reed's example, I walked over to the bookcase and slid my hands across the wood, feeling the scratches and indentations and even smelling the slight hint of smoke.

"Cool!" Jamie said. Then turning to me, he continued, "Can the bookcase go in my room since the desk is in your room?"

I laughed out loud. "Absolutely, Jamie. That is, if it's all right with Scott and Phyllis. They're part of this team too."

"It's definitely fine with us," Scott said. "Mom would never let us keep something like that in the house. She's too much of a neat freak, and something scratched and burned like that would never fit in. I think it's best if it stays with you."

Phyllis nodded in agreement.

"You know, though, that we'll be taking it to South Carolina with us when we leave next week, right?"

"We know," Scott said, "but it's still for the best. Besides, we'll keep in touch, won't we?"

For a moment, my joy was replaced with sorrow as I realized that we had only a few more days to spend with our new friends. Sure, Jamie and I had friends at home, but no one who could share in the adventures that we've had this summer. I couldn't think of anyone else I'd rather be solving mysteries with. Yes, I was truly going to miss Scott and Phyllis. Realizing I was about to cry, I mumbled, "Of course," in response to Scott's question and redirected my thoughts back to the bookcase.

"I guess we'll have to wait till Pop-Pop gets off work before we can come and get it," I said to Mr. Reed.

The storeowner shook his head. "No need. My team is out making deliveries today, and they'll be happy to load the bookcase into the truck and drive it over to your grandfather's house while they're out. It may take a couple of hours for them to arrive, but I would imagine that would still be quicker than waiting for your grandfather to get home from work. They can even unload it and set it up, if that's okay with you."

Okay? It was fantastic!

# CHAPTER SIXTEEN
## Dead End or New Beginning?

Wanting to ensure we were home when Mr. Reed's men arrived, we hurried back to Pop-Pop's house and waited for the anticipated delivery. Since it was such a lovely day, we decided to wait out back. Jamie was busy trying to get Watson to repeat his heroic performance from the night before so that Scott and Phyllis could see the results of Jamie's training. Watson, however, seemed more interested in playing with his toys and chasing various bugs around the yard. Watching him, I found myself wondering how in the world he had pulled off the ferocious tackle from the night before. It was obvious that the dog had an attention problem, sweet as he may be.

Scott and I sat in the lawn chairs in the shade of the porch awning. Scott seemed content to lie back and close his eyes, though I'm pretty sure he wasn't actually sleeping. Still, this worked out good for me because there were only a few pages left in Nathanael Greene's journal, and I was itching to read them. As our younger siblings played and Scott rested beside me, I settled in and opened the journal to where I had left off. As I read through the writing on the last page, I sat up straight.

"What is it?" Scott asked, noticing my posture and the shocked expression on my face.

"This is it," I said, pointing to the page before me. "This is the answer, well, at least one of the answers."

"Answers to what?" Phyllis asked, coming over and flopping down on the grass beside my chair. Even though we hadn't been outside long, she already carried the smell of sweat and dirt, but I resisted the urge to turn up my nose in disgust.

"You know how we found that letter from Lafayette, but we weren't sure what it was talking about?"

Scott and Phyllis nodded.

"Listen to this. *Though it wounds my honor, I have no choice but to seek aid from a friend. I cannot live a prisoner to this debt any longer. As fortune would have it, Lafayette predicted my downfall and made provisions for me when last he was here. In the letter I received from him today, he has left me the clues to where I can find the money he hid away for me. He assures me that it is enough to pay off my debts and more should additional misfortunes arrive. I am humbled by his generosity and feel a great sense of relief. To think, in just a few days my captivity will be over. Oh, the joy to see my sweet Caty's face when I tell her the news. She will be overjoyed, I think.*"

"What are you guys doing?" Jamie asked as he joined our huddle, bringing with him another waft of sweat and dirt.

"Reading about how Lafayette left money for Nathanael Greene," Scott said. "But I still don't get it. Greene died in debt, so does that mean he never found the fortune that Lafayette left?"

I studied the page again, searching through the text to find any clues, and even flipping through the next few empty pages to make sure I hadn't missed something. At first, I didn't see anything, but as I turned back to the original page, I noticed the date.

"He didn't have time to find it," I mumbled. "It says that this entry was written on June 11, 1786. Nathanael Greene died of a sunstroke eight days later, on his way home from a business trip to Savannah. I'm guessing he never had the chance to find the money that Lafayette left for him."

"What about his wife? Jamie asked. "Wouldn't she have gone after the money? I mean, wouldn't he have tried to tell her before he died?"

Shaking my head, I closed the book and hugged it to my chest. "I don't know, Jamie. Maybe he was waiting until he actually found the money before he told her, so as not to disappoint her if he didn't find it. But he waited too long, and he died before he had the chance to tell her or to find the money and pay off his debts."

"That's so sad," Phyllis mumbled.

I agreed completely. To think he was so close to setting things right and freeing himself from the bondage[22] of all that debt, but then he died at the young age of forty-four, thinking he had his whole life ahead of him.

The doorbell rang, interrupting my thoughts. Knowing that Pop-Pop didn't usually get many visitors, I jumped up in excitement, anticipating the delivery from Mr. Reed. The others followed closely on my heels as I sprinted to the foyer. When I opened the door, two men were standing there, one with a clipboard in hand.

"We have a delivery of a bookcase for Abby Patterson. Is this the right address?"

I nodded and clapped my hands together. "Yes, this is the place. I'm Abby."

The man studied the clipboard in his hand. "It says here we need to set it up for you as well. Where do you want it?"

Before I could answer, Jamie pushed past me. "It goes in my room. Come on, I'll show you the way."

Within a few moments, the new bookcase—or rather old bookcase—was in place in Jamie's room. After the delivery men had left, the four of us made our way back upstairs and crowded together around the piece of history. As I had done before, I ran my hands along the wood and studied the various notches and lines in the shelves, thinking that each one had a story to tell. But my thoughts were interrupted by Jamie, who seemed to be focused on a different part of the bookcase.

"These egg things sure are weird," he said, pointing to the emblems on the three doors at the bottom of the bookcase.

"Definitely!" Phyllis agreed, turning up her nose.

I studied the emblems carefully and found that I had to agree with my brother: they were very strange. They did, in fact resemble eggs, and I couldn't get around the fact that the etching reminded me of dragon skin. Suddenly, I realized something.

"Huh, that's odd."

"What's odd?" Scott asked, moving forward to stand beside me in front of the bookcase.

"Look at all three of the eggs. Each of the eggs is divided in half by a line. On these two," I said, gesturing toward the two outside cabinet doors, "the top half of the egg is smooth, and the bottom half looks like dragon skin." I looked into the faces of the others one by one to see if they understood what I was talking about. They each nodded, so I continued, pointing to the cabinet door in the middle. "But on this one, the top

I Once Was Lost                                                    135 half of the egg is like dragon skin, and the bottom half is smooth. Do you see what I mean? It's almost like it's upside down."

Scott, still nodding, said, "Yeah, I see what you mean, but is it possible that they did it differently because it was the center door, and they wanted it to be special?"

"It could be," I agreed, "or…"

"It could be a clue," Jamie interrupted, moving forward to stand just in front of the center cabinet door. "I've read about stuff like this in some of the books about the Masons. Sometimes they would build secret compartments into their furniture—like in your desk, Abby—and then they would place some sort of emblem that would open the secret door. A lot of times, all they had to do was turn the emblem the proper way, and the hidden door would open."

Reaching up with his right hand, Jamie took hold of the center egg and twisted. To my amazement, the emblem moved, and once it was turned right side up, I heard a faint click.

"Did you hear that?" Phyllis asked.

Nodding our heads, we all moved forward and studied the bookcase, looking for any secret compartments or open doors. It didn't take long.

"It's here!" Scott shouted from where he knelt on the floor, examining the bottom of the bookcase.

Under the three bottom cabinets, there was a piece of wood that I assumed was just some kind of molding like I had seen on other bookcases, but this one was definitely different. As Scott pushed against the bottom edge of the wood, the piece folded in like it was on a hinge, revealing a hidden compartment inside.

"Do you guys have a flashlight?" Scott asked. "It's dark in there, and I can't see anything."

Jamie reached into his front pocket. "Luckily for you, I have my top-secret detective flashlight right here." He withdrew a small flashlight and handed it to Scott. Unfortunately, there wasn't enough room for more than one person to look inside the secret compartment at once, and since Scott was the one who found it, it seemed only fair to let him look first."

Turning on the flashlight, Scott lowered his head to the floor and peered into the dark opening. "There's something in here," he said, reaching into the darkness. "I think it's a note of some kind."

He pulled out a yellowed piece of paper that looked familiar to me. "What is it?"

Still studying the dark opening, Scott reached behind him and handed the paper to me. After unfolding it, I stared at the rows of numbers, uncertain what it was I was looking at.

"What is it?" Jamie asked, crowding next to me to peer over my shoulder.

I turned the paper in his direction. "I'm not sure, but I think I recognize that handwriting." Running into my adjoining bedroom, I opened my nightstand drawer, and removed the letter from Lafayette that I had found in Nathanael Greene's journal. After returning to Jamie's room, I compared the two papers. Not only did the paper itself look identical, but there was no doubt about it that each of these letters was written by Lafayette.

"This must be the missing page from Lafayette's letter!" I shouted. "This is the clue to where he hid the fortune for Greene. If we can decipher[23] this, we might be able to find out where the money is."

Phyllis scrunched up her face and stared at the paper we had just discovered in the secret compartment of the bookcase. "Decipher what? It's just a bunch of numbers."

Jamie snapped his fingers. "No, it's a cipher."

"Like the ones we decoded from Greene's journal?" Scott asked as he rose from the floor and took the paper from Phyllis's hand.

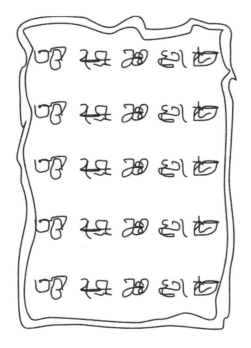

Jamie fumbled through the books on his nightstand. "Yes, just like those. Ciphers were secret messages written in code so that only those who knew how to decode the ciphers could read the message." Pulling a particular book from the stack, he flipped it open, and studied each page carefully, as if looking for something. "I know it's in here somewhere," he mumbled. "Aha, here it is!" he shouted, pointing to one of the pages.

Turning the book upside down so that the rest of us could see it, he pointed to a series of numbers on one of the pages. I had to admit that he was on to something.

Though the numbers were different, the overall set up was exactly the same. The numbers were arranged in five columns of three and stretched down the page for many rows. I felt it was safe to assume that the type of cipher was the same, but that didn't mean I had any clue how to solve it.

"Does the book say what all these numbers mean?" I asked Jamie.

Turning the book back to himself, he skimmed the pages, using his finger to draw an imaginary line down the page as he read. "It says here, *An Ottendorf cipher consists of three codes that corresponds to a random book or newspaper article. The first number corresponds to the page, the second number to the line on the page, and the third number to the letter/word in that line.*"

"So how does that help us?" Scott asked.

I studied the column of numbers again and shook my head. "I think it means we need to know which book or newspaper article is the key to solving the clue."

"But how will we know that?" Phyllis asked.

I turned to look at the bright-eyed girl. "I have no idea, but we have less than a week to figure it out before Jamie and I have to go back home to South Carolina."

# Glossary of Terms

—————————◆—————————

[1] ferocious - fierce, wild, violently cruel

[2] convulsed - shook violently

[3] abandoned - to leave or give up

[4] gaudy - very showy, usually in a bad way

[5] eclectic - chosen from many different sources; made up of items from various places

[6] stark contrast - very much unlike something else

[7] commissioned - made or brought into working condition

[8] hinder - to prevent; to cause delay, interruption or difficulty

[9] cosign - to sign a note or document belonging to someone else and taking responsibility for the terms of the agreement if the signers do not follow through

[10] ordeal - a trying or difficult situation

[11] grizzled - having gray or partly gray hair

[12] eerie - strange in a scary or creepy way

[13] duped - tricked; deceived

[14] frantic - wild with excitement or fear

[15] involuntary - not by one's own choice

[16] lolled - hung loosely; drooped; dangled

[17] closure - a conclusion; a sense of completeness

[18] hunkered - to hide or take shelter; to squat

[19] unobstructed - clear; not blocked from view

[20] Dr. Jekyll and Mr. Hyde - fictional characters by Robert Louis Stevenson; Dr. Jekyll was a scientist who created a potion to get rid of the wicked parts of himself, but instead, he ended up splitting himself into two personalities—one, the generous and compassionate Dr. Jekyll and the other, the mean and wicked Mr. Hyde.

# Glossary of Terms

[21] gist - the main or necessary part

[22] bondage - slavery; being under the control of something or someone else

[23] decipher - to figure out; to discover the meaning of

# History Hideout

---◆---

Are you curious about which historical facts in this book are true and which ones aren't?

Nathanael Greene was a true Revolutionary War hero who served the entire length of the war. He was under the command of George Washington and became good friends with the would-be president.

Lafayette was a Frenchman who was interested in the American fight for freedom and offered his money, his military knowledge and his connections in high places to aid the American army. He served, for a time, under Nathanael Greene. In fact, it was Greene who first felt that the young Frenchman was worthy of leading his own troops, so in that regard, Lafayette did owe Greene.

Sadly, all the information about Greene's debts is true. Due to poor choices and great misfortune, Greene died at a young age, never being able to repay all his debts.

Greene did have a campaign desk and matching bookcase made for him though whether or not he used them throughout the entirety of the war is anyone's guess. As for the secret compartments, that, too, is unknown though Greene was a Freemason, so it wouldn't be too farfetched to imagine that he had a few secrets here and there.

The journal? Well, it's possible that Greene had a personal journal, but if he did, I certainly don't know what happened to it or what kind of information it contained. All of the quotes in this book (unless attributed to Greene) were made up by the author for the sake of the story.

Did Lafayette leave behind a treasure? There are many rumors about a hidden treasure that Lafayette left behind, but there is no indication that the lost treasure had anything to do with Nathanael Greene. (But don't tell Abby and Jamie that, or there won't be a Book 5!)

If you want to know more about what's fact and what's fiction in the book, feel free to contact the author through the Delaware Detectives Readers' Club on Facebook or do some research of your own. There is a lot of information online, and I'm sure you can find several books at your local library.

# Cipher Center

———◆———

Cryptography is the use of codes and cyphers to create secret messages that can only be read by those who know how to break the code. As stated in the book, the Freemasons were a secretive society and were widely known for their use of a variety of ciphers. How are your decoding skills? See if you can figure out the messages below using some of the most popular ciphers. And don't forget what you learn here because you'll need it for the next book!

## Ottendorf Cipher (also known as the Book Cipher)

We covered this one in the book, but just in case you forgot, an Ottendorf cipher uses a particular book, poem or other piece of text and uses a set of numbers (typically groups of three) to indicate the key factors in decoding the message. For books, the numbers often referred to the page number, the line on the page and the word in that line. For example, 5-9-4 would mean that the next part of the clue was on page 5, the 9th line on the page, and the 4th word in that line. For shorter works, the three numbers corresponded to the line on the page, the word in that line and then the letter in that word. So, using the same code as above, 5-9-4, the clue would be on the 5th line, the 9th word on that line, and the 4th letter in that word. Make sense? Let's give it a try. To decode the message below, you'll need a King James Version of the Bible. Let's use the book of Psalms as our key, meaning the three-digit code will refer to the chapter, the verse, and then the word in the verse. Ready?

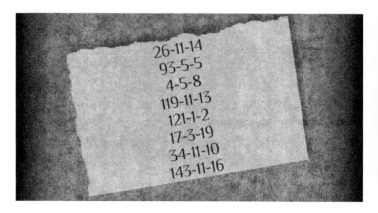

26-11-14
93-5-5
4-5-8
119-11-13
121-1-2
17-3-19
34-11-10
143-11-16

**Date Shift Cipher**

To use this system, the individuals need to decide on a date. Let's say, for example, that we use my birthday, 03/19/77. To create the cipher, write out the date without the slashes (031977), and write out the message you want to send. Under each letter of your message, write out your six-digit-code over and over again until you run out of letters. (See the example on the following page.)

# ILOVETOEATCHOCOLATE
# 0319770319770319770

Now, the number below each letter tells you how many letters to shift to the right to create your secret message. There is a "0" under the "I," which means it doesn't shift at all. The "L" shifts 3 places because it has a "3" underneath it, so in the new message the letter "L" will actually be "O" and so on. In the case of the letter "V," it would shift 9 letters to the right, which means you'll actually come back around to "A" and start over again (w,x,y,z,a,b,c,d,e). So "V" would now be "E." Your turn! See if you can figure out the message below using Nathanael Greene's date of birth: August 7,1742. (Hint: Your shift code will be 08071742.) Here's the message. To figure it out, use the shift code and count back *to the left* the appropriate number for each letter.

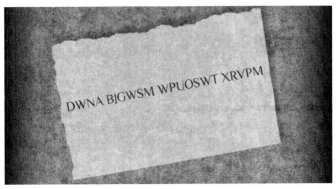

## Numbered Cipher

Decide upon a secret number that only you and the person receiving your message will know. For this example, let's use "7." Write out your message using only that many letters per line. So, using the code phrase I used earlier, "I love to eat chocolate," I would write out the message like this:

I L O V E T O
E A T C H O C
O L A T E

Now, to create our message, all we have to do is read down the columns and write the letters down in that order. The message now looks like this: IEALALOTAVCTEHETOOC. Knowing that the secret number is "7," the person receiving the message divides the number of letters in the message by 7 and finds out that there are 3 rows of letters. From there, it's simply a matter of writing out the letters one column at a time until there are 7 letters in each row (except for possibly the last row, as in our example). Let's see if you can figure out this message using the secret number "7." (Hint: There are 28 letters in the message, and all the rows will have 7 letters.)

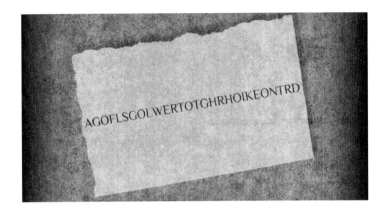

AGOFLSGOLWERTOTGHRHOIKEONTRD

## PigPen Cipher (also known as the Masonic Cipher)

These can be tough, but they're a lot of fun. To write and decode these messages, you'll need to create a special diagram that gives each letter of the alphabet a particular shape. Here's an example:

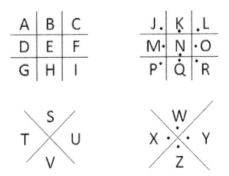

Once you've established the diagram you want to use, you write out your message using only the lines and dots surrounding the letters in the diagram. Are you ready to give it a try? Here's your message:

## Atbash Cipher (also known as Reverse Alphabet Cipher)

This is probably one of the easiest ciphers to write, but because of that, it's also the easiest to break. To create your message, write out the alphabet on one line and then write it backwards underneath it. It should look like this:

A B C D E  F G H  I  J  K L M N O P Q R S T  U V W X Y Z
Z Y X W V U T  S R Q P O N M L  K J  I  H G F  E D C B A

Now, write out your message, substituting the letters on the bottom for the letters on the top. In other words, "A" is now "Z" and "P" is "K." That's not too difficult, is it? Let's find out. Here's your message:

Z SZOU GIFGS RH Z DSLOV ORV

**Just in case you had trouble with the ciphers, here's the answer key:**

Ottendorf Cipher - Be sure your sin will find you out.

Date Shift Cipher - Don't accuse without proof.

Numbered Cipher - All things work together for good.

PigPen Cipher - Know what you believe.

Atbash Cipher - A half truth is a whole lie.

*The Delaware Detectives Readers' Club* is a place for children of all ages who enjoy good, clean mysteries. The discussions mainly center around *The Delaware Detective Mystery Series* by Dana Rongione (that's me).

This club will allow you to help me write the next books in the series. I want to hear from you. Have suggestions, comments or ideas? Let me know. In here, you'll get to help name the characters, describe the places, put together fun scenes and much more. There will be surveys, games, contests and lots of fun activities. And, if you love solving puzzles or unraveling clues, you'll love this place. So, check back often and see what's going on. As members of the club, you'll also be the first people to get to read the book, and I'll put your names in the front of the book for all to see. How cool is that?

If you haven't read **The Delaware Detectives** books, that's okay. You're still welcome to join the group, but I'm also happy to tell you that you can get the first book in the series for free on Amazon. Just follow this link: http://amzn.to/2bWkNiO

To join the *Delaware Detectives Readers' Club,* search for the group on Facebook and click the "join" button to gain permission to join the group. Once permission has been granted, you'll be able to read the posts about past and upcoming books, as well as ask questions, make suggestions and join in the fun and games when they take place.

I look forward to chatting with you there!

# About the Author

Dana Rongione is the author of several Christian books, including the highly-praised **Giggles and Grace** devotional series for women. A dedicated wife and doggie "mom," Dana lives in Greenville, SC, where she spends her days writing and reaching out to the hurting and discouraged.

Connect with her at <u>DanaRongione.com</u>, sign up for her daily devotions, and support her ministry at https://www.patreon.com/DRongione.

# Books by Dana Rongione

**Devotional/Christian Living:**
He's Still Working Miracles
There's a Verse for That
'Paws'itively Divine: Devotions for Dog Lovers
The Deadly Darts of the Devil
What Happened To Prince Charming?:
Understanding What To Do When You No Longer
Know the Man You're Married To
*Giggles and Grace Series:*
  Random Ramblings of a Raving Redhead
  Daily Discussions of a Doubting Disciple
  Lilting Laments of a Looney Lass
  Mindful Musings of a Moody Motivator

**Other Titles for Adults:**
Improve Your Health Naturally
Creating a World of Your Own: Your Guide to
Writing Fiction

**The Delaware Detectives Middle-Grade Mystery Series:**
Book #1 – The Delaware Detectives: A Middle-Grade Mystery
Book #2 – Through Many Dangers
Book #3 – My Fears Relieved
Book #4 – I Once Was Lost

**Books for Young Children:**
Through the Eyes of a Child
God Can Use My Differences

**Audio:**
Moodswing Mania – a Bible study through select
Psalms (6 CD's)
The Names of God – a 6-CD Bible study exploring
some of the most powerful names of God
Miracles of the Old Testament, Part 1 – a Bible study
with a unique look at miracles in the Old Testament
(4 CD's)
There's a Verse for That – Scripture with a soft
music background, perfect for meditation or
memorization

For more information about Dana's books and ministry
outreach, visit DanaRongione.com.

Printed in Great Britain
by Amazon

19417473R00098